8/98

THE FABER BOOK OF
FAVOURITE FAIRY TALES

ff

The Faber Book of
FAVOURITE
FAIRY TALES

Edited by
Sara and
Stephen Corrin

Illustrated by
Juan Wijngaard

faber and faber
LONDON · BOSTON

First published in 1988
by Faber and Faber Limited
3 Queen Square London WC1N 3AU

Photoset by Parker Typesetting Service Leicester
Printed in Hong Kong by Mandarin Offset Ltd

All translations except for 'East o' the Sun and West o' the Moon',
'Cinderella' and 'Thorn Rose, the Sleeping Beauty'
© Sara and Stephen Corrin, 1988
Translations of 'Cinderella' and 'Thorn Rose, the Sleeping Beauty'
© Lucy Meredith, 1988

Illustrations © Juan Wijngaard, 1988

British Library Cataloguing in Publication Data

The Faber book of favourite fairy tales.
1. Tales – Anthologies – For children
I. Corrin, Sara   II. Corrin, Stephen
III. Wijngaard, Juan
398.2'1

ISBN 0-571-14854-9

to Julia, Eve and
TOM

Sources of the Stories

'Hansel and Gretel', 'The Goose-Girl', 'Rapunzel', 'Little Red Riding Hood', 'Snow-White and the Seven Dwarfs', 'Thorn Rose, the Sleeping Beauty', 'The Frog Prince', 'Rumpelstiltskin' and 'The Twelve Dancing Princesses' are from *Fairy Tales* (*Kinder und Hausmärchen*) by the Brothers Grimm; 'Cinderella', 'Bluebeard' and 'Puss in Boots' from *Fairy Tales* (*Histoires ou Contes du Temps Passé*) by Charles Perrault; 'The Ugly Duckling', 'The Princess on the Pea', 'Thumbelina' and 'The Emperor's New Clothes' from *Fairy Tales* (*Samlede Eventyr og Historier*) by Hans Christian Andersen; 'Baba Yaga, the Bony-legged, the Witch' from *Russian Fairy Tales* (*Russkie Narodnye Skazki*) by Aleksandr Afanasiev; 'Aladdin and the Wonderful Lamp' and 'Ali Baba and the Forty Thieves' from *The Thousand and One Nights*, a translation of *The Arabian Nights* by Antoine Galland; 'East o' the Sun and West o' the Moon' from *Popular Tales from the Norse (Fairy Tales and Folk Legends)* (*Norske Folke Eventyr*) by P. C. Asbjörnsen and Jorgen I. Møe; 'The Three Wishes' and 'Beauty and the Beast' from *The Three Wishes* and *Beauty and the Beast* by Madame le Prince de Beaumont, from *Le Magasin des Enfans*; 'Jack and the Beanstalk' and 'The Three Sillies' from *English Fairy Tales* by Joseph Jacobs; 'Midas and the Golden Touch' from *The Metamorphoses* by Ovid, *Myths of Ancient Greece retold for Young People* by Robert Graves and *A Wonder Book* by Nathaniel Hawthorne. Our thanks are due to the Victoria and Albert Museum and to the British Library for allowing us to use material connected with 'The Story of the Three Bears' which is available only there.

All translations are by Stephen Corrin, except 'East o' the Sun and West o' the Moon' (translated by Sir George Webbe Dasent), 'Cinderella' and 'Thorn Rose, the Sleeping Beauty' (both translated by Lucy Meredith). We have used the English titles by which the stories are best known today.

Contents

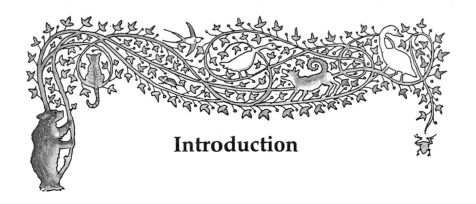

Introduction

Fairy tales recount the mysterious pranks and adventures of supernatural spirits who manifest themselves in the form of (often diminutive) human beings and other creatures. They possess the power to regulate the affairs of men for good or evil according to their deserts.

All peoples have created their own myths, but perhaps all are drawn from the same sources, or originate in those predicaments which are inseparable from the human condition.

In Oscar Wilde's *The Devoted Friend* Linnet asks Rat to listen to a story on the subject of friendship. 'Is it about me?' asks Rat, 'because if it is, I'll listen, for I'm mighty fond of fiction.'

Fairy tales do indeed speak to our deepest selves and this is perhaps why they go direct to the heart of the child. One five-year-old gets right to the nub of a complex little drama: in his own re-telling of 'Rumpelstiltskin', he reassures us listeners – or is it himself he is reassuring? – with the words, 'Don't worry, the queen does keep the baby.' The magic of these stories is their very essence. 'In magic,' a six-year-old told us, 'just about anything can happen, even if it's absolutely impossible, like you could get to Buckingham Palace in a jiffy.' It accords perfectly with the children's own fantasy; they have taken hold of these fantasies and will not let them go.

Do we need yet more fairy tales? The point is, they are not *more* to children. Children are *new* and these stories are *new* to children. If they *have* heard them once, they will need to hear them over and over again. And each time they will take fresh delight in them, discovering new wonders and at the same time finding out more about themselves and their fellow beings.

Anatole France, a distinguished scholar in the fields of myth and antiquity, contemplating his own fifteen-week-old 'miracle of a child' and anticipating the joy of sharing those magical tales which had become so much a part of him with this small creature, wrote, 'I will tell her all manner of tales and she will become madly in love with them.'

We hope that this present beautiful edition of the world's best-loved fairy tales (and our *own* favourites), exquisitely illustrated by Juan Wijngaard, will also make young readers fall in love with them.

The Opies' *Classic Fairy Tales*, which has become an internationally celebrated source-book, gives the very first translations of these stories to appear in English. We, on the other hand, have sought out the first published versions, recorded by the greatest creators and collectors of tales – Perrault, Grimm, Afanasiev, Andersen, Madame le Prince de Beaumont and Asbjörnsen – and made our *own* translations of almost all of them. Two versions by Lucy Meredith, 'Cinderella' (from Perrault) and 'Thorn Rose' (from Grimm), have been included for their sheer beauty and elegance, while the translation of Asbjörnsen's 'East o' the Sun and West o' the Moon' is by Sir George Webbe Dasent and is the best-known version of that remarkably lovely story.

The two tales from *The Arabian Nights* we have translated from the text of Professor Antoine Galland, whose French rendering of these exotic stories (*Les Mille et Une Nuits*) was the route by which they came to Europe from the Orient. These stories are often extravagantly protracted, so we have taken the liberty of trimming their length while retaining much of the Oriental embroidery.

'Midas and the Golden Touch' is based on the text in Ovid's *Metamorphoses*, with added touches from Robert Graves and a whisper or two from Nathaniel Hawthorne. A brief note precedes Robert Southey's 'The Three Bears'.

Some collections of fairy tales pre-date those mentioned

above – those of Straparola (1550) and Basile (1634–6) and those of Hindu, Greek and Norse origin. A version of 'Cinderella' going back to over a thousand years was found recorded in India. The Zulus and Maoris have likewise provided us with tales with the same universal themes as many of those in this present collection. No fewer than 365 variants of the 'Cinderella' theme have been identified.

Why indeed have such strikingly similar themes been discovered in almost every corner of the earth? The incidents, objects and characters in these stories cannot but symbolize the emotional experiences of all people, whether primitive or civilized. They must also reflect the frailty and precariousness of our existence, as well as our struggles and aspirations.

Children have a rough sense of justice, and it is a matter of constant amazement that this seems to come to the fore earlier than other aspects of their intellectual and affective development. Motives, in particular, seem to exercise their imagination – this despite the opinions of experts who keep insisting that until the age of ten or eleven children are not capable of assimilating motive as part of their moral diet. Of course, in fairy tale the good are *very* good and the bad go to the extremes of inhumanity and cruelty. Small wonder then that we sometimes find the endings of these tales unduly savage.

Walter de la Mare as a child could gaze without fear into Bluebeard's dreaded cupboard; he could watch the barrel with the queen nailed inside it roll down into the sea. But he remembered stories in which the violence was introduced for its own sake, and he *hated* them. He was as sure as one could be that not one of *those* tales was a fairy tale.

Little Kitya, three and a half years of age, in Chukovsky's work *Two to Five*, told her father, 'I know you're going to tell me that there aren't any Baba Yagas, but I want a story *with* a Baba Yaga.' A seven-year-old loved the line in which Baba Yaga gnashes her iron teeth. It was frightening, she thought, 'but I loved it best.' And of 'Rumpelstiltskin', 'it was so exciting, I just didn't know what to do. I thought I'd burst out laughing or crying or something.'

Walter de la Mare's son told his father, who was trying to reassure him that there were no bears under his bed or anywhere in England for that matter, 'The trouble is, Daddy, it's not a real bear.'

'Since it's inevitable,' said C. S. Lewis, 'that they will meet evil, let them also meet brave knights and heroes who overcome their enemies. Their inner fears and fantasies must find some outer expression.'

The stories presented in this volume are rock-firm and their spell cannot be broken, whatever changes the future may bring. Since children today are fed on a diet of television entertainment that reflects our modern world so blatantly and powerfully, it is salutary that anthologies of these immortal classics should continue to be presented to them.

Sara and Stephen Corrin

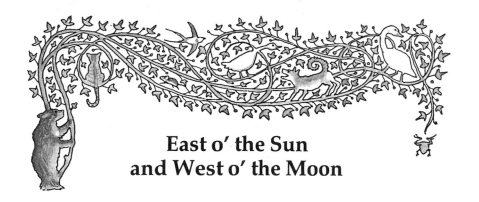

East o' the Sun
and West o' the Moon

Once upon a time there was a poor husbandman who had so many children that he hadn't much of either food or clothing to give them. Pretty children they all were, but the prettiest was the youngest daughter, who was so lovely there was no end to her loveliness.

So one day, 'twas on a Thursday evening late at the fall of the year, the weather was so wild and rough outside, and it was so cruelly dark, and rain fell and wind blew, till the walls of the cottage shook again. There they all sat round the fire busy with this thing and that. But just then, all at once something gave three taps on the window-pane. Then the father went out to see what was the matter; and, when he got out of doors, what should he see but a great big White Bear.

'Good evening to you!' said the White Bear.

'The same to you,' said the man.

'Will you give me your youngest daughter? If you will, I'll make you as rich as you are now poor,' said the Bear.

Well, the man would not be at all sorry to be so rich; but still he thought he must have a bit of a talk with his daughter first; so he went in and told them how there was a great White Bear waiting outside, who had given his word to make them rich if he could only have the youngest daughter.

The lassie said 'No!' outright. Nothing could get her to say anything else; so the man went out and settled it with the White Bear, that he should come again the next Thursday evening and get an answer. Meantime he talked his daughter over, and kept on telling her of all the riches they would get, and how well off she would be herself; and so at last she thought better of it, and washed and mended her rags, made herself as smart as she could, and was ready to start. I can't say her packing gave her much trouble.

Next Thursday evening came the White Bear to fetch her, and she got upon his back with her bundle, and off they went. So, when they had gone a bit of the way, the White Bear said –

'Are you afraid?'

No! she wasn't.

'Well! mind and hold tight by my shaggy coat, and then there's nothing to fear,' said the Bear.

So she rode a long, long way, till they came to a great steep hill. There, on the face of it, the White Bear gave a knock, and a door opened, and they came into a castle, where there were many rooms all lit up; rooms gleaming with silver and gold; and there too was a table ready laid, and it was all as grand as grand could be. Then the White Bear gave her a silver bell; and when she wanted anything, she was only to ring it, and she would get it at once.

Well, after she had eaten and drunk, and evening wore on, she got sleepy after her journey, and thought she would like to go to bed, so she rang the bell; and she had scarce taken hold of it before she came into a chamber, where there was a bed made, as fair and white as any one would wish to sleep in, with silken pillows and curtains, and gold fringe. All that was in

2

the room was gold or silver; but when she had gone to bed, and put out the light, a man came and laid himself alongside her. That was the White Bear, who threw off his beast shape at night; but she never saw him, for he always came after she had put out the light, and before the day dawned he was up and off again. So things went on happily for a while, but at last she began to get silent and sorrowful; for there she went about all day alone, and she longed to go home to see her father and mother, and brothers and sisters. So one day, when the White Bear asked what it was that she lacked, she said it was so dull and lonely there, and how she longed to go home to see her father and mother, and brothers and sisters, and that was why she was so sad and sorrowful, because she couldn't get to them.

'Well, well!' said the Bear, 'perhaps there's a cure for all this; but you must promise me one thing, not to talk alone with your mother, but only when the rest are by to hear; for she'll take you by the hand and try to lead you into a room alone to talk; but you must mind and not do that, else you'll bring bad luck on both of us.'

So one Sunday the White Bear came and said now they could set off to see her father and mother. Well, off they started, she sitting on his back; and they went far and long. At last they came to a grand house, and there her brothers and sisters were running about out of doors at play, and everything was so pretty, 'twas a joy to see.

'This is where your father and mother live now,' said the White Bear; 'but don't forget what I told you, else you'll make us both unlucky.'

No! bless her, she'd not forget; and when she had

4

reached the house, the White Bear turned right about and left her.

Then when she went in to see her father and mother, there was such joy, there was no end to it. None of them thought they could thank her enough for all she had done for them. Now, they had everything they wished, as good as good could be, and they all wanted to know how she got on where she lived.

Well, she said, it was very good to live where she did; she had all she wished. What she said besides I don't know; but I don't think any of them had the right end of the stick, or that they got much out of her. But so in the afternoon, after they had done dinner, all happened as the White Bear had said. Her mother wanted to talk with her alone in her bedroom; but she minded what the White Bear had said, and wouldn't go upstairs.

'Oh! what we have to talk about, will keep,' she said, and put her mother off. But somehow or other, her mother got round her at last, and she had to tell her the whole story. So she said, how every night, when she had gone to bed, a man came and lay down beside her as soon as she had put out the light, and how she never saw him because he was always up and away before the morning dawned; and how she went about woeful and sorrowing, for she thought she should so like to see him, and how all day long she walked about there alone, and how dull and dreary and lonesome it was.

'My!' said her mother; 'it may well be a Troll you slept with! But now I'll teach you a lesson how to set eyes on him. I'll give you a bit of candle, which you can carry home in your bosom; just light that while he is asleep, but take care not to drop the tallow on him.'

5

Yes! she took the candle, and hid it in her bosom, and as night drew on, the White Bear came and fetched her away.

But when they had gone a bit of the way, the White Bear asked if all hadn't happened as he had said?

Well, she couldn't say it hadn't.

'Now, mind,' said he, 'if you have listened to your mother's advice, you have brought bad luck on us both, and then, all that has passed between us will be as nothing.'

No, she said, she hadn't listened to her mother's advice.

So when she reached home, and had gone to bed, it was the old story over again. There came a man and lay down beside her; but at dead of night, when she heard he slept, she got up and struck a light, lit the candle, and let the light shine on him, and so she saw that he was the loveliest prince one ever set eyes on, and she fell so deep in love with him on the spot, that she thought she couldn't live if she didn't give him a kiss there and then. And so she did, but as she kissed him, she dropped three hot drops of tallow on his shirt, and he woke up.

'What have you done?' he cried; 'now you have made us both unlucky, for had you held out only this one year, I had been freed. For I have a stepmother who has bewitched me, so that I am a White Bear by day, and a Man by night. But now all ties are snapped between us; now I must set off from you to her. She lives in a castle which stands east o' the sun and west o' the moon, and there, too, is a princess, with a nose three ells long, and she's the wife I must have now.'

She wept and took it ill, but there was no help for it; go he must.

Then she asked if she mightn't go with him?

No, she mightn't.

'Tell me the way, then,' she said, 'and I'll search you out; *that* surely I may get leave to do.'

Yes, she might do that, he said; but there was no way to that place. It lay east o' the sun and west o' the moon, and thither she'd never find her way.

So next morning, when she woke up, both prince and castle were gone, and there she lay on a little green patch, in the midst of the gloomy thick wood, and by her side lay the same bundle of rags she had brought with her from her old home.

So when she had rubbed the sleep out of her eyes, and wept till she was tired, she set out on her way, and walked many, many days, till she came to a lofty crag. Under it sat an old hag, and played with a gold apple which she tossed about. Her the lassie asked if she knew the way to the prince who lived with his stepmother in the castle that lay east o' the sun and west o' the moon, and who was to marry the princess with a nose three ells long.

'How did you come to know about him?' asked the old hag; 'but maybe you are the lassie who ought to have had him?'

Yes, she was.

'So, so; it's you, is it?' said the old hag. 'Well, all I know about him is, that he lives in the castle that lies east o' the sun and west o' the moon, and thither you'll come, late or never; but still you may have the loan of my horse, and on him you can ride to my next neighbour. Maybe she'll be able to tell you; and when you get there, just give the horse a switch under the left ear, and beg him to be off home; and, stay, this gold apple you may take with you.'

7

So she got upon the horse, and rode a long long time, till she came to another crag, under which sat another old hag, with a gold carding-comb. Her the lassie asked if she knew the way to the castle that lay east o' the sun and west o' the moon, and she answered, like the first old hag, that she knew nothing about it, except it was east o' the sun and west o' the moon.

'And thither you'll come, late or never, but you shall have the loan of my horse to my next neighbour; maybe she'll tell you all about it; and when you get there, just switch the horse under the left ear, and beg him to be off home.'

And this old hag gave her the golden carding-comb; it might be she'd find some use for it, she said. So the lassie got up on the horse, and rode a far far way, and a weary time; and so at last she came to another great crag, under which sat another old hag, spinning with a golden spinning-wheel. Her, too, she asked if she knew the way to the prince, and where the castle was that lay east o' the sun and west o' the moon. So it was the same thing over again.

'Maybe it's you who ought to have had the prince?' said the old hag.

Yes, it was.

But she, too, didn't know the way a bit better than the other two. 'East o' the sun and west o' the moon it was,' she knew – that was all.

'And thither you'll come, late or never; but I'll lend you my horse, and then I think you'd best ride to the East Wind and ask him; maybe he knows those parts, and can blow you thither. But when you get to him, you need only give the horse a switch under the left ear, and he'll trot home by himself.'

And so, too, she gave her the gold spinning-wheel.

'Maybe you'll find a use for it,' said the old hag.

Then on she rode many many days, a weary time, before she got to the East Wind's house, but at last she did reach it, and then she asked the East Wind if he could tell her the way to the prince who dwelt east o' the sun and west o' the moon. Yes, the East Wind had often heard tell of it, the prince and the castle, but he couldn't tell the way, for he had never blown so far.

'But, if you will, I'll go with you to my brother the West Wind, maybe he knows, for he's much stronger. So, if you will just get on my back, I'll carry you thither.'

Yes, she got on his back, and I should just think they went briskly along.

So when they got there, they went into the West Wind's house, and the East Wind said the lassie he had brought was the one who ought to have had the prince who lived in the castle east o' the sun and west o' the moon; and so she had set out to seek him, and how he had come with her, and would be glad to know if the West Wind knew how to get to the castle.

'Nay,' said the West Wind, 'so far I've never blown; but if you will, I'll go with you to our brother the South Wind, for he's much stronger than either of us, and he has flapped his wings far and wide. Maybe he'll tell you. You can get on my back, and I'll carry you to him.'

Yes! she got on his back, and so they travelled to the South Wind, and weren't so very long on the way, I should think.

When they got there, the West Wind asked him if he could tell her the way to the castle that lay east o' the sun and west o' the moon, for it was she who ought to have had the prince who lived there.

9

'You don't say so! That's she, is it?' said the South Wind. 'Well, I have blustered about in most places in my time, but so far have I never blown; but if you will, I'll take you to my brother the North Wind; he is the oldest and strongest of the whole lot of us, and if he doesn't know where it is, you'll never find any one in the world to tell you. You can get on my back, and I'll carry you thither.'

Yes! she got on his back, and away he went from his house at a fine rate. And this time, too, she wasn't long on her way.

So when they got to the North Wind's house, he was so wild and cross, cold puffs came from him a long way off.

'BLAST YOU BOTH, WHAT DO YOU WANT?' he roared out to them ever so far off, so that it struck them with an icy shiver.

'Well,' said the South Wind, 'you needn't be so foul-mouthed, for here I am, your brother, the South Wind, and here is the lassie who ought to have had the prince who dwells in the castle that lies east o' the sun and west o' the moon, and now she wants to ask you if you ever were there, and can tell her the way, for she would be so glad to find him again.'

'YES, I KNOW WELL ENOUGH WHERE IT IS,' said the North Wind; 'once in my life I blew an aspen leaf thither, but I was so tired I couldn't blow a puff for ever so many days after. But if you really wish to go thither, and aren't afraid to come along with me, I'll take you on my back and see if I can blow you thither.'

Yes! with all her heart; she must and would get thither if it were possible in any way; and as for fear, however madly he went, she wouldn't be at all afraid.

'Very well, then,' said the North Wind, 'but you

must sleep here tonight, for we must have the whole day before us, if we're to get thither at all.'

Early next morning the North Wind woke her, and puffed himself up, and blew himself out, and made himself so stout and big, 'twas gruesome to look at him; and so off they went high up through the air, as if they would never stop till they got to the world's end.

Down here below there was such a storm; it threw down long tracts of wood and many houses, and when it swept over the great sea, ships foundered by hundreds.

So they tore on and on – no one can believe how far they went – and all the while they still went over the sea, and the North Wind got more and more weary, and so out of breath he could scarce bring out a puff, and his wings drooped and drooped, till at last he sunk so low that the crests of the waves dashed over his heels.

'Are you afraid?' said the North Wind.

No! She wasn't.

But they weren't very far from land; and the North Wind had still so much strength left in him that he managed to throw her up on the shore under the windows of the castle which lay east o' the sun and west o' the moon; but then he was so weak and worn out, he had to stay there and rest many days before he could get home again.

Next morning the lassie sat down under the castle window, and began to play with the gold apple; and the first person she saw was the Long-nose who was to have the prince.

'What do you want for your gold apple, you lassie?' said the Long-nose, and threw up the window.

'It's not for sale, for gold or money,' said the lassie.

11

'If it's not for sale for gold or money, what is it that you will sell it for? You may name your own price,' said the princess.

'Well! if I may get to the prince, who lives here, and be with him tonight, you shall have it,' said the lassie whom the North Wind had brought.

Yes! she might; that could be done. So the princess got the gold apple; but when the lassie came up to the prince's bedroom at night he was fast asleep; she called him and shook him, and between whiles she wept sore; but for all she could do she couldn't wake him up. Next morning as soon as day broke, came the princess with the long nose, and drove her out again.

So in the daytime she sat down under the castle windows and began to card with her golden carding-comb, and the same thing happened. The princess asked what she wanted for it; and she said it wasn't for sale for gold or money, but if she might get leave to go up to the prince and be with him that night, the princess should have it. But when she went up she found him fast asleep again, and for all she called, and for all she shook, and wept, and prayed, she couldn't get life into him; and as soon as the first grey peep of day came, then came the princess with the long nose, and chased her out again.

So, in the daytime, the lassie sat down outside under the castle window, and began to spin with her golden spinning-wheel, and that, too, the princess with the long nose wanted to have. So she threw up the window and asked what she wanted for it. The lassie said, as she had said twice before, it wasn't for sale for gold or money; but if she might go up to the prince who was there, and be with him alone that night, she might have it.

Yes! she might do that and welcome. But now you must know there were some Christian folk who had been carried off thither, and as they sat in their room, which was next the prince, they had heard how a woman had been in there, and wept and prayed, and called to him two nights running, and they told that to the prince.

That evening, when the princess came with her sleepy drink, the prince made as if he drank, but threw it over his shoulder, for he could guess it was a sleepy drink. So, when the lassie came in, she found the prince wide awake; and then she told him the whole story how she had come thither.

'Ah,' said the prince, 'you've just come in the very nick of time, for tomorrow is to be our wedding day; but now I won't have the Long-nose, and you are the only woman in the world who can set me free. I'll say I want to see what my wife is fit for, and beg her to wash the shirt which has the three spots of tallow on it; she'll say yes, for she doesn't know 'tis you who put them there; but that's a work only for Christian folk, and not for such a pack of Trolls, and so I'll say that I won't have any other for my bride than the woman who can wash them out, and ask you to do it.'

So there was great joy and love between them all that night. But next day, when the wedding was to be, the prince said –

'First of all, I'd like to see what my bride is fit for.'

'Yes!' said the stepmother, with all her heart.

'Well,' said the prince, 'I've got a fine shirt which I'd like for my wedding shirt, but somehow or other it has got three spots of tallow on it, which I must have washed out; and I have sworn never to take any other bride than the woman who's able to do that. If she can't, she's not worth having.'

Well, that was no great thing, they said, so they agreed, and she with the long nose began to wash away as hard as she could, but the more she rubbed and scrubbed, the bigger the spots grew.

'Ah!' said the old hag, her mother, 'you can't wash; let me try.'

But she hadn't long taken the shirt in hand, before it got far worse than ever, and with all her rubbing, and wringing, and scrubbing, the spots grew bigger and blacker, and the darker and uglier was the shirt.

Then all the other Trolls began to wash, but the longer it lasted, the blacker and uglier the shirt grew, till at last it was black all over as if it had been up the chimney.

'Ah!' said the prince, 'you're none of you worth a straw: you can't wash. Why there, outside, sits a beggar lassie, I'll be bound she knows how to wash better than the whole lot of you. Come in, lassie!' he shouted.

Well, in she came.

'Can you wash this shirt clean, lassie, you?' said he.

'I don't know,' she said, 'but I think I can.'

And almost before she had taken it and dipped it in the water, it was as white as driven snow, and whiter still.

'Yes; you are the lassie for me,' said the prince.

At that the old hag flew into such a rage, she burst on the spot, and the princess with the long nose after her, and the whole pack of Trolls after her – at least I've never heard a word about them since.

As for the prince and princess, they set free all the poor Christian folk who had been carried off and shut up there; and they took with them all the silver and gold, and flitted away as far as they could from the castle that lay east o' the sun and west o' the moon.

P. C. ASBJÖRNSEN *and* JORGEN I. MØE

The Ugly Duckling

It was glorious out in the country. It was summer. The corn was golden yellow, the oats were green, the hay was stacked up in the green meadows and the stork walked around on his red legs chattering in Egyptian, a language he had learned from his mother. All around the fields and meadows there were woods and in the midst of these woods were deep lakes. Yes indeed, it was glorious out in the country.

Standing there in the sunshine was an old manor, surrounded by a deep moat, and from its walls right down to the water's edge grew great dock leaves, which were so tall that small children could stand upright under the tallest of them; it was as wild here as in the thickest wood. And a duck was sitting there on her nest, hatching out her little ducklings. But she was getting tired; it was taking such a long time and hardly anyone ever came to pay her a visit. The other ducks preferred to swim about in the water rather than sit under a dock leaf chatting to her.

At last the eggs began to crack one after the other – peep! peep! peep! All the egg yolks had come alive and were popping their heads out.

'Quack! Quack!' said the mother duck and they all hurried out as fast as they could, blinking their little eyes all around them under the green leaves. And Mother Duck let them look to their hearts' content, for green is good for the eyes.

'What a big world it is!' cheeped all the little ones, for they now had much more room than when they were in the eggs.

'Don't go thinking that this is the whole world!' said their mother. 'It stretches far beyond the other side of the garden right into the vicarage, though I've never been that far myself . . . Well, are you all here?' And she stood up. 'No, I haven't got you all yet, the biggest egg is still there. How long is that one going to take, I wonder. I'm just about fed up with waiting!' And she sat down on it again.

'Well, how goes it?' inquired an old duck, who was paying her a call.

'There's this one egg here. It's taking an awfully long time,' said the mother duck. 'I just can't get it to hatch. But come and have a look at the others. They are the loveliest ducklings you have ever set eyes on. They're the image of their wretched father, who never comes to see me.'

'Just let me have a look at the egg that won't hatch,' said the old duck. 'Yes, I thought so. You may take my word for it, that's a turkey's egg, all right! I was fooled once like that myself! And I had my pack of troubles with the young ones, I can tell you! They're afraid of the water. I just couldn't get them to go in! I quacked and clucked, but a fat lot of good that did! Just let me see that egg again. Yes, to be sure, that's a turkey's egg, all right! I'd just leave it, if I were you, and teach the other ones to swim.'

'Ah well, I think I will sit on it a bit longer,' said the duck. 'I've sat so long, a few days more won't make any difference.'

'It's no concern of mine,' said the old duck and off she waddled.

17

At last the great egg did burst. 'Peep! Peep!' said the new-born duck, tumbling out. My! he certainly was big and ugly! Mother Duck looked at him. 'He's quite appallingly large!' said she. 'None of the others looked anything like that! Surely, he couldn't be a turkey-chick! Anyway, we'll soon find out! He's going to go into the water even if I have to kick him in myself!'

The next day the weather was perfect and the sun shone down on all the green dock leaves. Mother Duck and all her family came down to the water. Splash! and in she went. 'Quack, quack!' she clucked and in went the ducklings one after the other. The water closed over their heads but up they came again straight away and swam delightfully. Their little legs worked busily away; they were all in the water, even the grey ugly one.

'No, he's no turkey,' she said. 'Look how well he moves his legs, how upright he holds himself! He's my very own child and no mistake, and he's really quite pretty when you take a second look at him. Come along, all of you now, follow me and I'll take you out into the great wide world and introduce you to the other members of the duckyard. But stay close to me all the time or you may get trodden on. And beware of the cat!'

And so out they all went into the duckyard, where there was a terrible row going on between two families quarrelling over an eel's head. But the cat got it in the end.

'Well, that's how things are in the world,' said the mother duck, her mouth watering a little, for she would dearly have loved the eel's head for herself. 'Now come along, use your legs properly and don't dilly-dally, and when you pass that old duck over there, be sure to bow your heads politely, for she is the most distinguished person here. She has Spanish blood in her veins, that's why she's so fat. And can you see? She has a red band of cloth round her leg, which means she's somebody very special, and it's the greatest distinction a duck can enjoy. It signifies that she's somebody we can't do without, somebody who is looked up to by both men and animals. Come on now! Smarten yourselves up a bit! You must *not* turn your toes in. Well-bred ducklings don't do that, they keep their legs well apart, just like father and mother. Now bow your heads politely and say, "Quack!"'

And this they did. The other ducks looked round and stared at them and said, loud enough for every-body to hear, 'Now we've got this lot to put up with! There's far too many of us here as it is! And whew! just look at that one over there! We're certainly not going to stand for him!' And one duck flew right over to him and bit him in the neck.

'Now you just leave him alone, d'you hear!' said the mother duck. 'He hasn't done anything to you!'

'Yes, but just look at the size of him!' said the duck who had bitten him. 'And he certainly *looks* odd! He had best be kept in his place!'

'That's a pretty lot of ducklings,' said the old duck with the red cloth band round her leg. 'All of them, that is, except that ugly thing there. He's not a success, is he? It's a pity you can't hatch him out all over again!'

'I'm afraid there's nothing can be done about it, Your Grace,' said the mother duck. 'He's none too pretty to look at but he's extremely good-natured, and he's as good a swimmer as any of the others – a little better, even, I dare say. Perhaps he'll grow up less ugly in time and not look quite so gawky. He was in the egg too long, that's his trouble, and it has had an effect on his shape.' Then she gave him a peck on the neck and smoothed his feathers. 'Anyway,' she added, 'looks don't matter all that much because he's a drake. He'll turn out all right in the end, he's sturdy enough.'

'The other ducklings are presentable enough,' said the old duck. 'Well, make yourselves at home, and if you happen to find an eel's head, I'd be grateful if you'd bring it along to me.'

And so they made themselves at home. But the wretched little duck which was the last to be hatched and which looked so clumsy was bitten and pushed around and made to look silly both by the ducks and the chickens. 'He is too big,' they all said. And the turkey cock, who had been born with spurs and therefore considered himself an emperor, puffed himself out like a ship in full sail and came straight at him, gobbling for all he was worth and getting almost purple in the face. The wretched duckling didn't know where he dared stand or walk and felt quite miserable because he looked so ugly and was the laughing stock of the whole yard.

As the days went by things got worse and worse. The poor duckling was chased around by everyone and even his own brothers and sisters turned nasty towards him. 'If only the cat could get at you!' they kept saying and his mother said, 'I wish you'd get right out of my sight.' The ducks bit him, the chickens pecked him and the girl who fed the poultry never missed giving him a kick.

One day he ran off and flew over the fence, but the little birds in the bushes also made off in terror. 'It's because I'm so ugly,' thought the duckling and he shut his eyes and flew on farther till he came out on to the great moor, where the wild ducks lived. Here he lay the whole night through, tired and sick at heart.

When he woke up next morning, he saw a whole flock of wild ducks come flying towards him.

'What may you be?' they asked, looking the new-comer up and down, and the duckling bowed his head in greeting, turning his head this way and that, as best he could.

'You *are* ugly and no mistake,' they said, 'but we don't care as long as you don't marry into our family.' Oh, the poor little thing! His thoughts were very far from marrying. All he hoped for was to be allowed to lie in the sedge and drink a little marsh water.

He lay in those marshes for two long days and then along came two wild geese (or rather, two wild ganders, for they were both he-geese). It hadn't been all that long since they'd been hatched and that is, perhaps, why they said the first thing that came into their heads.

'Listen, friend,' they said, 'you are so ugly we've quite taken to you. Why not come along with us and be a bird of passage? Close by in the next moor there are some delightful wild geese, all waiting to marry and all able to cackle beautifully. Come along and try your luck. Ugly as you are, you might make a hit.'

Just at that moment there were two loud bangs and the two wild geese fell down dead in the rushes and the water became red with their blood. Then there were two further shots and whole flocks of wild geese rose up from among the reeds. Then there was another loud report. A great hunt was going on, there were huntsmen lying in wait all around the marshes, and some were perched among the branches of the

overhanging trees. Blue gunsmoke rose up like clouds into the dark trees and drifted away slowly over the water. Retriever dogs came splashing their way through the swamp, bending the reeds and rushes in all directions. It was all terribly frightening for the poor duckling; he tried to hide his head under his wing but just at that moment a menacingly big dog came nosing right up to him. Its tongue hung out of its mouth, its eyes gleamed most fearfully and it thrust its muzzle right into the duckling's face, showing its sharp, dangerous teeth and then . . . splash! off it bounded without doing any harm to the frightened little creature.

'Thank God!' sighed the duckling. 'I am so ugly even the dog can't be bothered to bite me.'

And so he lay perfectly still as the gunshots whistled through the reeds and the banging and shooting deafened his ears. Not till late in the day did it become quiet again, but the duckling didn't dare move from the spot where he lay. After waiting several hours he raised his head from under his wing, looked about him and hurried off out of the marsh as fast as he could. Over field and meadow he ran on and on, though a fierce storm had begun to rage so that he had great difficulty in making his way.

Towards evening he came to a broken-down little hut. It was in such a tumbledown state that it didn't know which side to fall and so it remained standing. The wind blew so fiercely that the poor duckling had to sit back on his tail to stop himself being blown away; but the storm got worse and worse. Then he noticed that the door had come off one of its hinges and slanted in such a way as to leave a gap through which he could slip inside. And this he did.

It so happened that an old woman lived in this wretched little hut with her cat and her hen. The cat was called Sonnykins and he could arch his back and purr, and his fur would even give out sparks if you stroked him the wrong way. The hen was called Chick Shortykins because of her ridiculously short legs, but she was a good layer and the old woman was very attached to her.

In the morning they very soon noticed that there was a strange duckling in the house, and the cat began to purr and the hen to cackle.

'What's all this then?' said the woman, looking around, but she couldn't see all that well and so she thought the duckling was some nice fat duck that had lost its way.

'Ah!' she said, 'that's a nice little thing we've caught. Now I'll be able to get some duck eggs, that is, if it's not a drake! We'll soon tell.'

And so the duckling was taken on trial for three weeks – but no eggs appeared. The cat was master of the house and the hen the mistress. '*We* – and the rest of the world,' they used to say, as if nobody else mattered. The duckling was not too sure about this, but the hen kept him firmly in his place.

'Can you lay eggs?' she asked.

'No.'

'Then kindly hold your tongue.'

And the cat said, 'Can you arch your back, can you purr and can you flash sparks?'

'No.'

'Then kindly refrain from expressing opinions when sensible folk are talking.'

So the duckling sat in a corner feeling as sad as sad could be. He thought of the fresh air and the sunshine and felt a sudden longing to swim on the water – so strong was the feeling he had to tell the hen about it.

'What on earth has come over you?' asked the hen. 'All these odd notions come into your silly head because you just sit and don't do anything! Lay an egg or purr or something, and you'll soon feel yourself again, I assure you.'

'But it's really so lovely in the water,' said the duckling. 'It's grand getting the water over your head and plunging right down to the bottom.'

'Oh yes, it must be really grand!' said the hen. 'You're crazy, that's what you are! Ask the cat, there's nobody cleverer than he is. Just you ask him whether *he* likes swimming in the water and plunging down to the bottom. And don't ask me what *I* think. Better still, ask your mistress, the old woman. She is certainly the cleverest person in the world. Do you think she has any inclination to go swimming in the water and letting it close all over her head?'

'You don't understand what I mean,' said the duckling.

'Well, if *we* can't understand you, who on earth would, I'd like to know! I suppose you fancy yourself cleverer than the cat or the old woman, not to mention me! Get rid of those fancy ideas, child! And show some gratitude for all the kindness that's been shown to you! Haven't you been fortunate to find a warm room and company you can learn something from? No, you are just a chatterbox. It's no fun associating with the likes of you! Believe me, what I'm telling you is for your own good. I'm telling you a few unpleasant truths, that's the sign of a genuine friend. Come on, now! Make an effort, lay some eggs and learn to purr and give out sparks!'

'I think I'll go out into the wide world,' said the duckling.

'Yes, you do that,' said the hen.

So the duckling went off and swam in the water and dived deep down, but all creatures kept away from him because he was so ugly.

By now it was autumn. The leaves in the forest turned yellow and brown and the wind whirled them round and round in an untidy dance. Up in the clouds it looked cold and the air was heavy with hail and snowflakes and on the fence stood the raven and squawked out of sheer cold; it made you feel chillier than ever. The poor duckling felt thoroughly miserable.

One evening, against a glorious sunset, a whole flock of handsome birds arose out of the bushes; never had the duckling witnessed anything so beautiful. Dazzlingly white they were, with long graceful necks. They were swans, of course, and, with a singularly strange cry, they spread their splendid wide wings and flew off to warmer faraway lands where the lakes do not freeze. Higher and higher they flew and the ugly little duckling felt a strange longing as he watched them. He wheeled round and round in the water, stretched out his neck in the air towards them and gave out such a peculiar cry that he himself was frightened by it. Oh, he could never forget those beautiful, blesséd birds. When they were out of sight he plunged right to the bottom of the water and when he came up again he felt stranger than ever. He did not know the name of those birds nor where they were flying but he loved them more than anything else he had ever loved before. He wasn't the least bit envious of them – such loveliness was not meant for him. He would have been happy if only the ducks had allowed him into their company – the poor, wretched creature!

And the winter was bitterly cold. The duckling had to swim about in the water to stop it from freezing up entirely. But every night the hole where he swam became smaller and smaller. It froze and the crust of ice crackled, and the duckling had to use his legs constantly to stop the ice from closing in on him. In the end he became quite exhausted and lay quite still, frozen fast in the ice.

Early the next morning a farm worker happened to pass by and spotted him. He went out to him and broke the ice with his wooden shoe and carried the duckling back home to his wife. There he came to life again. His children wanted to play with him but the duckling thought they might do him harm and in his terror flew straight into the milk vat, sending a shower of milk all over the room. The woman screamed and clapped her hands and the duckling flew into a tub where the butter was and from there into a barrel of flour and out again. You can just imagine what a sight he must have looked after all this! The woman was screeching her head off and threw the tongs at him. The children, laughing and yelling, tripped over one another as they tried to catch him. Luckily the door happened to be open and the poor thing was able to fly out into some bushes amid the newly fallen snow. And there he lay as though in a trance.

It would be too sorrowful a tale to tell you all that the poor duckling had to go through during that harsh winter. He lay out in the swamp among the reeds until at last the sun began to shine again and the larks to sing. It was a magnificent spring.

Once more the duckling stretched his wings,

beating the air more vigorously than before, and flew strongly away. And before he could feel the full pleasure of it, he found himself in a large garden full of apple trees in bloom and scented lilac trees whose long green branches hung down over the winding canals. How gloriously beautiful it was here, so full of the freshness of spring! And what is this coming towards him out of the thickets? Three beautiful white swans, their feathers rustling, gliding ever so smoothly over the water! The duckling recognized those splendid creatures and felt overcome by a strange melancholy.

'I will fly over to those royal birds,' he thought to himself, 'and perhaps they will put me to death for daring to come near them in all my ugliness. But that does not matter. Better to be killed by them than be bitten by ducks, pecked at by hens, chased by the girl who feeds the poultry, or to go hungry through another winter.' He flew out into the water and swam towards the beautiful swans. They saw him and came sailing swiftly towards him with rustling wings. 'Only kill me,' said the poor creature and he bowed his head low against the flat of the water, expecting death. But what was this that he could see in the clear water? He saw beneath him his own image, but no longer that of a clumsy, ugly, grey bird. What he beheld was a snow-white swan! It doesn't really matter if you are born in a duckyard, as long as you've been hatched from a real swan's egg!

And now he somehow felt happy that he had been through all those troubles and hardships, for he could feel a greater joy in all the loveliness and good fortune that was ahead of him. The splendid swans swam slowly round him and stroked him with their beaks. Little children came running into the garden and threw bread and corn into the water. The smallest exclaimed, 'Look, there's a new one!' And the others shouted delightedly, 'Yes, a new one has arrived!' They clapped hands and danced around and ran to their mothers and fathers, and more bread and cake were thrown into the water. 'This new one is the most beautiful of them all,' they said, 'he's so young and handsome!' And the old swans bowed their heads to him.

Then he felt quite shy and covered his head with his wings; he was so happy, he didn't know what to do with himself. But he was not proud, for a kind heart is never proud. And he kept thinking how he had been ill-treated and despised, and now he could hear them all saying that he was the most beautiful of all the birds! The elder tree bent down its branches over the water before him, and the sun shone warm and bright. He rustled his feathers, raised his slender neck and in the joy of his heart he thought, 'Little did I dream of such great happiness when I was the Ugly Duckling!'

HANS CHRISTIAN ANDERSEN

Hansel and Gretel

At the edge of a great forest there once lived a poor woodcutter with his second wife and his two children, a boy named Hansel and a girl named Gretel. They were so poor they had hardly a bite to eat, and when a great famine came over the land they found they were down to their very last crumb. One night when the man lay in bed, thinking and worrying and tossing and turning, he gave a heavy sigh and said to his wife, 'What's going to become of us? How can we feed the children when we haven't even got enough for ourselves?'

'I know what,' said his wife. 'We'll take the children out into the woods very early in the morning – into the thickest part of the woods – we'll light a fire for them and give them each a morsel of bread, then we'll go off to our work and leave them there alone. They'll never find their way back home and so we'll be shot of them.'

'No, wife,' said her husband, 'that I will *not* do. How could I find it in my heart to abandon my children in the woods? Wild beasts would come and tear them to pieces.'

'What a fool you are!' said his wife. 'Must all four of us die of hunger? You'd better start smoothing up the boards for our coffins', and she went on scolding him until, with a heavy heart, he gave in.

Now the two children hadn't been able to fall asleep because they were so hungry, and they'd heard what their stepmother had said to their father. Gretel wept bitter tears and said to Hansel, 'So that's what's going to happen to us.'

'Now, now, Gretel, be calm,' said Hansel, 'don't worry, I'll find a way out.' And when his parents were asleep he got up, put on his jacket, opened the lower part of the door and slipped out. The moon was shining, and the white pebble-stones that lay in front of the house gleamed bright and clear like so many silver coins. Hansel bent down and stuffed as many of them as he could into his jacket pocket. Then he went back into the house and said to Gretel, 'Rest assured, little sister, God will not forsake us. Have a good sleep.' And then he himself got back into his bed.

At daybreak, even before the sun had risen, the woman came and woke up the two children. 'Get up, lazybones, we've got to be off to the forest to gather wood.' Then she gave each of them a morsel of bread, saying, 'That's something for your dinner, but don't eat it too soon because you'll not be getting any more.' Gretel tucked the bread away under her apron, because Hansel's pockets were full of pebbles. Then they all set off together along the path that led to the forest. After a little while, Hansel stopped and looked back towards the house, and he kept doing this again and again.

'Hansel, what are you doing, looking back and stopping all the time?' said his father. 'Just keep up with us and watch where you are going.'

'Oh, Father,' said Hansel, 'I'm looking back at my little white cat, sitting up there on the roof trying to say goodbye to me.'

31

'Silly child,' said the woman. 'That's no cat, it's the morning sun shining on the chimney.'

But Hansel hadn't been looking at the cat; he'd been taking one of the white pebbles out of his jacket and throwing it down on the path every time he stopped.

When they came to the middle of the forest the father said, 'Now, children, you gather some wood. I'll get a fire going so that you don't freeze.' So Hansel and Gretel gathered a pile of brushwood, and made a heap hill-high. When the fire was lit and the flames were leaping up, the woman said, 'Now, children, lie down and rest by the fire while we go further into the forest to chop wood. We'll come back and fetch you when we've finished.'

Hansel and Gretel sat by the fire, and when it was midday they ate their little bits of bread. And because they could hear the blows of an axe, they thought their father must be somewhere nearby. But it wasn't the axe but a branch that their father had tied to a withered old tree so that it kept banging to and fro in the wind. And after they had sat there for a pretty long while, their eyes closed from sheer weariness and they fell asleep.

When they awoke at last, it was already well into the night and very dark. Gretel began to weep again. 'How are we ever going to get out of this forest?' she said. Hansel comforted her. 'Just wait a little while till the moon rises,' he said, 'and then we'll find our way all right.'

And indeed, when the full moon had risen, Hansel took his little sister by the hand and turned back to follow the trail of the pebble-stones, which gleamed like new-minted silver coins to show them the way home. They walked all through the night and arrived at

32

their father's house at daybreak. They knocked at the door, and when the woman opened it and saw Hansel and Gretel standing there, she said, 'What wicked children you are! What were you up to, sleeping so long in the woods? We thought you were never coming back.' Their father, however, was overjoyed, because he'd been heartbroken at leaving them alone and abandoned.

It wasn't very long before famine struck again in every corner of the land. The children overheard their stepmother say to their father in bed at night, 'We've come to the end of everything we've got; there's just about a half a loaf left and when that's gone, then that will be the end of it. The children will have to be sent off; we'll lead them deeper into the woods, so they'll never find the way out again. Otherwise there's no hope for us.' The man's heart ached to hear this and he thought to himself, 'Surely it would be better if we shared our last bite with the children.' But whatever he had to say, his wife wouldn't listen, she scolded him and swore at him. And as he who says 'A' must also say 'B', so it was with him. As he had given in the first time, he now had to give in the second time as well.

But the children were awake all the time and had heard all their talk. So Hansel got up again while they were still asleep, intending to pick up pebble-stones as he'd done before. But the woman had locked the door, so he couldn't get out. He comforted his little sister, saying, 'Don't cry, Gretel, go on sleeping, God will surely help us.'

Early next morning the woman came and got the children out of bed. She gave them each their bit of bread, which was even smaller than the first morsel.

33

Along the path on their way to the forest Hansel broke up the bread in his pocket and kept stopping to throw crumbs on to the ground to make a trail.

'Hansel,' said his father, 'why do you keep stopping and looking round? Just look where you're going.'

'I'm looking back at my little dove,' said Hansel. 'It's sitting on the roof saying goodbye to me.'

'Silly boy,' said the woman, 'that's not your dove, it's the morning sun shining on the chimney.' But bit by bit Hansel scattered all his crumbs along the path.

The woman led the children still deeper into the woods, where they had never been in all their born days. And there another big fire was kindled and the stepmother said, 'You children just stay and sit here, and when you feel tired you may have a little sleep. We'll be off to chop wood, and in the evening, when we've finished, we'll be back to fetch you.'

As it was now midday, Gretel shared her bread with Hansel, for he had strewn his along the path. Then they fell asleep, and the evening went by, but no one came for those poor children. It was dark and far into the night before they awoke, and Hansel comforted his little sister, saying, 'Just wait till the moon comes up and then we shall see the breadcrumbs that I threw down and they'll show us the way back home.' They got up when the moon came out, but they didn't find any breadcrumbs, for the many thousands of birds that fly around in the woods and fields had pecked them up.

'We'll find the way all the same,' Hansel told Gretel, but they did not find it. They walked all night long, and then the next day from morning till night, but they did not find their way out of the forest, and they were very hungry, for they had eaten nothing but the berries scattered on the ground. And since they were so very weary that their legs could carry them no further, they lay down under a tree and fell asleep.

And now it was the third morning since they had left their father's house. They started walking again, but they went deeper and deeper into the woods and if help didn't come soon they must surely perish.

About midday they saw a beautiful little bird, as white as snow, perched on a branch and singing so beautifully that they stopped to listen. And when it had finished it took wing and flew off in front of them, and they followed it until they came to a little house, where it perched itself on the roof. And then, as they came quite close they saw that the house was built of bread, with cakes as a roof, and windows made of transparent sugar.

'Let's have a real feast. I'll eat a piece of the roof and you have some of the windows, Gretel, they look tasty enough.' Hansel reached up and broke off a little of the roof to see what it tasted like, and Gretel went and stood by the window-panes and took a few bites. And just then a little voice called out from somewhere in the room:

> Nibble, nibble, nindow,
> Who's nibbling at my window?

And the children answered:

> It's the wind a-blowing,
> A-sighing and a-soughing.

And then they went on eating, taking no notice of the voice.

Hansel, who found the roof really tasty, broke off a

35

large piece of it, while Gretel pushed out a whole round slab of window-pane and sat herself down to enjoy it. Suddenly the door opened and an old woman, as old as the hills, came limping out on a crutch. Hansel and Gretel had such a terrible fright that they dropped the food they were holding in their hands, but the old woman shook her head and said, 'Well, well, dear little children, and who's brought you here? Come along inside and stay with me, there's nothing to be afraid of.' She grasped both of them by the hand and led them into her little house. Then they were served with plenty of good food, milk and pancakes with sugar, apples and nuts. And after that two beautiful little beds, all clean and white, were prepared for them, and Hansel and Gretel got in and thought they were in heaven.

But the old woman had only been pretending to be kind. She was really a wicked witch who lay in wait for children and had built the eatable house simply to lure them in. Once a child was in her power, she would cook it and eat it, and that for her would be a real feast-day. Witches have red eyes and can't see very far, but they have a fine sense of smell, as keen as that of animals, and they soon notice when human beings are near them. When Hansel and Gretel came close to her little house she gave an evil laugh and said gloatingly, 'Well, I've got these all right, and they won't get away.'

Early next morning, before the children were awake, she got up, and when she saw them both, looking so pretty as they slept, she muttered to herself, 'They'll make a nice mouthful.' Then she grasped Hansel with her scrawny hand and carried him to the little stable and locked him in behind a grilled gate. He could shout as much as he liked, it wouldn't do him any good. Then she went to Gretel, shook her awake and cried, 'Get up, lazybones, fetch water and cook something good for your brother out there in the stable, so he can get nice and fat. And when he is fat, I'm going to eat him up.' Gretel began to weep bitterly, but it wasn't any use; she had to do what the wicked witch required.

So now Hansel had all the best food cooked for him, while Gretel got nothing but crab-shells. Every morning the old woman would hobble down to the stable and call out, 'Hansel, stretch your little finger out, so I can feel if you're getting fat enough.' But Hansel would put out a little bone, and the old woman, whose eyes were dim, couldn't see it properly and thought it was Hansel's finger and was puzzled that he wasn't even starting to get fatter. When four weeks had passed and Hansel seemed as thin as ever, impatience got the better of her and she couldn't wait any longer.

'Hey, there, Gretel,' she called to the girl. 'Look smart and fetch some water. Fat or thin, tomorrow I'm going to butcher Hansel and boil him.' Oh dear, dear! How his poor little sister wept and wailed when she had to carry the water, big tears rolling down her cheeks.

'Dear God, help us!' she cried. 'If only the wild beasts had eaten us up in the woods, we should at least have died together.'

'That's quite enough of your blubbering,' snapped the old woman, 'it won't get you anywhere.'

Early next morning Gretel had to go out, fill the cauldron with water and get the fire alight.

'First we'll do the baking,' said the old woman. 'I've already heated the oven and kneaded the dough.' She

37

pushed poor Gretel outside to the oven, from which flames were already pouring.

'You get inside there,' said the witch, 'and see that it's getting heated up properly, so we can shoot the bread in.'

She meant to push Gretel into the oven and roast her, so that she could eat her too. But Gretel guessed just what she had in mind and said, 'I don't quite know how to do it. How do I get inside?'

'Silly goose,' said the old woman, 'the opening is big enough. Just look, I could get in there myself.' And she twisted about and stuck her head into the oven. Then Gretel gave her a mighty push so that she fell right in, closed the iron door and dropped the bar down.

Then she rushed to the stable, opened the door and cried, 'Hansel, we are saved! The old witch is dead!'

Then Hansel sprang out, like a bird from a cage when the door is opened. How overjoyed they were! They couldn't stop hugging each other, kissing and jumping about. And since they had nothing more to fear, they went into the witch's house, where they found caskets of pearls and precious stones in every corner.

'These are even better than pebble-stones,' said Hansel, and he stuffed as many as he could into his pockets. And Gretel said, 'I'd like to take something back home, too,' and she filled her apron full.

'But now we'd better be off,' said Hansel, 'so that we can get away from this bewitched wood.' But after they had been walking for a few hours they came to a great stretch of water.

'We won't get across this,' said Hansel. 'I can't see a way across anywhere and there's no bridge.'

'And there's no boat either,' said Gretel, 'but look, there's a little white duck swimming over there. Perhaps if I ask her she will help us.' So she called out:

> *Little white Duck, oh dear little Duck,*
> *We're rid of the witch, but here we're stuck,*
> *Pray take us across on your soft downy back.*
>
> *And the duck replied with a friendly quack.*

Then the duck swam up to them. Hansel got on her back and asked Gretel to join him.

'Oh no,' answered his sister, 'that would be too heavy for her. She'll take us one at a time.' And that's just what the kind little creature did. When they were happily across on the other side and had walked on a little while, the woods seemed to look more and more familiar, until at last they espied their father's house in the distance. Then they began to run, burst into the house and smothered their father with hugs and kisses. The poor man had not had a moment's peace of mind since he had left them in the woods. As for the wicked stepmother, she had died.

Gretel shook out her apron, and the pearls and precious stones came leaping out into the room, while Hansel turned one handful after another out of his pockets. So now all their cares were at an end and there was nothing to mar their happiness.

THE BROTHERS GRIMM

The Goose-Girl

Long ago there lived a queen whose husband had died long since and who had a beautiful daughter. When she grew older she was promised to a king's son who lived far away in a distant land. Now when the time came for them to be married and the girl had to journey to an unknown kingdom, the queen packed up the most costly utensils and jewellery, gold and silver and goblets and precious trinkets, in short, everything that should form part of a royal bridal dowry, for she loved her child most dearly. She also sent a chambermaid to travel with her and escort the bride to the bridegroom. Each of them was given a horse for the journey – but the princess's horse, called Falada, could talk.

When the time came for them to leave, the mother went up to her bedchamber and with a little knife cut her fingers so they bled. Then she held a little piece of white cloth under the fingers so that three drops of blood fell on to it, and she gave the cloth to her daughter, saying, 'My dear child, take great care of this, for you may find that you will need it on your journey.'

And so they bade each other a sorrowful farewell. The princess tucked the little cloth in her bosom, mounted her horse and set off to her bridegroom. After they had been riding for about an hour, she felt a burning thirst and she told her chambermaid, 'Pray get down and, with my cup that you've brought along for me, scoop up some water from the stream. I'd dearly love to have a drink.'

'If you are thirsty,' said the maid, 'get down yourself, lie down by the water and drink. I don't care to be your servant any longer.' So the princess, desperate with thirst, got off her horse, bent over the water of the stream and drank; no golden goblet for her.

'Oh God!' she sighed, and as she did so, the three drops of blood answered:

> *If this thy mother only knew,*
> *It would break her heart in two.*

But the royal bride was a humble girl; she said nothing, and remounted her horse. And so they rode on a few miles, but the weather was warm, the sun beat down, and soon she felt parched with thirst again. As they came to a river, she once more called to her chambermaid, 'Pray get down and fetch me something to drink in my golden goblet,' for she had long forgotten the saucy words the maid had spoken before. But the chambermaid, more haughty than ever, replied, 'If you want a drink, get it yourself. I will not be your servant.'

The princess dismounted, her raging thirst leaving her no choice, and bending over the flowing water, she wept and cried, 'Oh God!' And the drops of blood once more replied:

> *If this thy mother only knew,*
> *It would break her heart in two.*

But as she drank and leaned right over the water,

41

the little cloth with its three drops of blood slipped from her bosom and was carried away down the stream. And she, poor girl, in her great sorrow, did not even notice it. But the chambermaid *had* seen it and rejoiced at the power she now had over the bride, for once the blood-drops were lost the princess was weak and defenceless.

The princess got up and was about to mount her horse again, when the maid said, 'I'm the one to ride on Falada now, and you can take the old nag that I've been riding on,' and the princess had to put up with that too. Then, with harsh words, the chambermaid ordered her to take off all her royal robes and put on her own drab ones instead, and finally, she had to swear in the name of heaven that she would tell nothing of all this at the royal court. And if she had not taken this oath, she would have been murdered there and then. But Falada saw all this and took good note of it.

So the chambermaid now mounted Falada and the true bride got on the old nag, and thus they rode on their way. At last they arrived at the royal castle. There was great rejoicing at their coming, and the prince sprang forward to meet them and lifted the chambermaid from her horse, believing her to be his bride. She was led up the steps while the princess was left standing below. But the old king, looking out of the window, saw her standing in the courtyard and noted how delicate she was, how gentle-looking and how very beautiful. So straight away he went to the royal chamber and there he inquired of the bride about the girl she had with her, standing down there in the courtyard: who might *she* be?

'It's someone I've brought with me for company on the journey. Give her some work to do – she doesn't have to stand doing nothing down there.'

The old king was at a loss to think of anything, but then he said, 'Well, there is a young boy who looks after the geese; perhaps she could help him.' The boy was known as Kurdkin, and the true bride was given the job of helping him look after the geese.

Shortly afterwards the false bride said to the young prince: 'Dearest one, I beg you to do me a favour.' The prince replied, 'Your wish is my command.'

'Well then,' she said, 'let the knacker be sent for so that he may cut off the head of that horse on which I rode hither; it annoyed me one way or another all the way here.' In reality, though, she was afraid that the horse might tell how she had changed places with the princess, and for fear of that, the faithful Falada must die.

But word of this came to the ears of the true princess, and she secretly promised the knacker a piece of gold if he would do a small service for her. In the town there was a tall, dark archway through which she had to take the geese every morning and evening. The knacker was to hang up Falada's head under this dark archway so that she might be able to see him again and again. And this the knacker promised to do. He hacked off the horse's head and nailed it under the dark archway.

Early in the morning, as Kurdkin and the princess drove the geese through the arch, she said:

Alas, poor Falada, there thou hangest.

And the head answered:

Alas, poor princess, there thou gangest.
If this thy mother only knew,
It would break her heart in two.

43

Then she was silent as they drove the geese out beyond the town and into the fields. And when she came to the meadow, she seated herself on the grass and let down her hair, which shone like pure gold. And young Kurdkin, when he saw it, was enchanted to see how it glistened and wanted to pull out a couple of locks. And she said:

> Blow, blow, blow, little wind, today.
> Blow young Kurdkin's cap away.
> Blow it here and blow it there
> Till I've braided up my golden hair.

And then there blew up such a strong wind that it carried young Kurdkin's cap far into the countryside and he had to chase after it. By the time he'd got back she had finished her combing and plaiting, so there wasn't a single hair he could get hold of. This made young Kurdkin angry and he wouldn't talk to her. And so they tended the geese together till evening and then went back home.

The next morning, as they were driving the geese out under the dark archway, the girl said:

> Alas, poor Falada, there thou hangest.

And the head answered:

> Alas, poor princess, there thou gangest.
> If this thy mother only knew,
> It would break her heart in two.

And again, once they were in the fields, she sat down in the pasture and began combing out her hair, which made young Kurdkin run up and try to pull

some out. But she said quickly:

> *Blow, blow, blow, little wind, today.*
> *Blow young Kurdkin's cap away.*
> *Blow it here and blow it there*
> *Till I've braided up my golden hair.*

Then the wind blew and blew his little cap far off, so that young Kurdkin had to chase after it, and by the time he came back she had long tidied her hair and he had no chance of getting a single strand of it. And so they went on looking after the geese until evening.

But in the evening, after they had reached home, young Kurdkin went before the old king and said, 'I will no longer look after the geese with that girl.'

'And why is that?' asked the old king.

'Because she does nothing but annoy me all day long,' he replied.

So the old king ordered him to tell what went on between him and her, and young Kurdkin said, 'When we go through the dark archway in the mornings, there's a nag's head up there on the wall and she says to it:

> *Alas, poor Falada, there thou hangest.*

And the head answers:

> *Alas, poor princess, there thou gangest.*
> *If this thy mother only knew,*
> *It would break her heart in two.*

And then he went on to tell what happened in the goose-meadow and how he had to keep running after his little cap when it was blown away by the wind.

46

Then the old king ordered him to drive out the geese again the next morning, and the king himself sat behind the dark archway and heard the goose-girl talking to Falada's head. Then he followed her on to the field and hid behind a bush in the meadow. And he soon saw with his own eyes how the goose-girl and the goose-boy drove the flock of geese along and how, after a while, she sat upon the grass and let down her tresses, which shone like gold. And straight away she said once more:

> *Blow, blow, blow, little wind, today.*
> *Blow young Kurdkin's cap away.*
> *Blow it here and blow it there*
> *Till I've braided up my golden hair.*

Then there came a gust of wind that carried away young Kurdkin's little cap and made him run miles to get it, while the girl quietly combed and plaited her hair. The king observed all this and went back home unnoticed. But when evening came he called the goose-girl to his side and asked her what it all meant.

'I'm not permitted to tell you that, nor may I tell any man of my sorrow, for so have I sworn under the open sky. Otherwise I should have perished.'

The king pressed her to tell and left her no peace, but he could get nothing from her. So he said, 'Well, if you cannot tell me, go and tell your sorrows to the iron stove,' and he went away.

Then she crept into the iron stove and began to wail and weep; she poured out her heart and spoke: 'Here I sit now, abandoned by the whole world, and yet I am a king's daughter, and a false chambermaid forced me to lay aside my royal clothes, and has taken my place beside my bridegroom, while I must do the common tasks of a goose-girl. If this my mother only knew, it would break her heart in two.'

But the old king was standing outside by the stove-pipe, waiting and listening to what she was saying. And now he came back into the room and bade her get out of the stove. Then she was given royal garments to put on and it seemed a miracle how beautiful she was. The old king called his son and revealed to him that he had taken a false bride: she was simply a chamber-maid, the true one was standing there – the one-time goose-girl.

The young prince was filled with joy when he saw how beautiful and truly good she was. A great feast was arranged to which all important people and good friends were invited. At the head of the table sat the bridegroom, the princess on one side of him and the chambermaid on the other. But the chambermaid was quite blinded by the splendour of it all and no longer recognized the other girl in her dazzling adornments.

When they had all eaten and drunk and were feeling in high spirits, the old king set the chambermaid a riddle: What should become of such and such a person who had, in such and such a manner, betrayed her master – and he recounted the whole course of events. 'What punishment does such a person deserve?'

The false bride replied, 'She deserves nothing better than to be taken out, stark naked, and stuck in a barrel lined inside with sharp nails, and then, drawn by two white horses, be led from street to street till she dies.'

'You are that traitress,' said the old king. 'You have pronounced your own sentence and you will be dealt with accordingly.'

And once this sentence was carried out, the young

prince was wedded to his rightful bride and they both ruled their kingdom in peace and happiness.

THE BROTHERS GRIMM

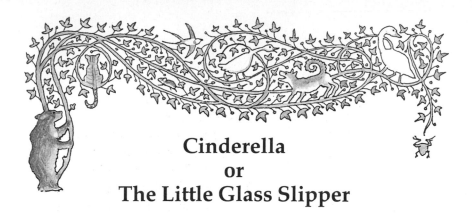

Cinderella
or
The Little Glass Slipper

Once upon a time there was a gentleman who married for the second time. His new wife was a very proud, haughty woman, and her two daughters were exactly like her. Her husband had a daughter of his own, a girl of wonderful goodness and gentleness. She took after her mother, who had been a most lovable person.

The wedding was hardly over when the stepmother's bad temper broke out. Her stepdaughter's charm infuriated her, because it made her own daughters seem even more unlikeable by comparison. She made the girl do the roughest housework; she had to wash the dishes and scrub the stairs and clean the rooms of the mistress of the house and her lady daughters. She slept at the top of the house, in an attic, on a thin straw mattress, while her sisters had rooms with polished floors and beds in the latest fashion and mirrors where they could see themselves from head to foot. The poor girl endured it all and dared not complain to her father, who would only have scolded her, because he was entirely dominated by his wife.

When she had finished her work she used to sit among the ashes in the chimney corner, and so most people in the house called her Cinders. The younger stepsister, who was not as ill-natured as the elder, called her Cinderella. And in spite of her ugly old clothes Cinderella was a hundred times more beautiful than her sisters in their magnificent dresses.

One day the king's son gave a ball and invited everyone of importance. The two sisters were asked, for they were much sought after. They were delighted, and very busy choosing the dresses and hairstyles that would suit them best. It all meant more work for Cinderella, who had to press their linen and goffer their cuffs. They couldn't talk about anything but what they were going to wear at the ball.

'I shall wear my red velvet embroidered dress,' said the elder sister.

'I must make do with my old skirt,' said the younger one, 'but still, I shall wear my cloak with flowers of cloth of gold and my diamond necklace, so I shan't do badly.'

They sent for a famous hairdresser to arrange their head-dresses and they bought patches from the most fashionable maker. They called Cinderella to ask her opinion, for she had good taste. She gave them excellent advice, and even offered to do their hair, which they were very glad to agree to.

While she was doing it, they said to her, 'Cinderella, would you like to go to the ball?'

'You are teasing me, ladies. It wouldn't be suitable.'

'You're quite right; it would make everyone laugh to see Cinders at the ball.'

Anyone but Cinderella would have made their hair look hideous, but she was a kind-hearted girl and she did it perfectly. They were so excited that they could hardly eat for two days. They broke more than twelve laces in pulling in their corsets to make their waists look smaller and they were always in front of the mirror.

At last the great day came. They set out and Cinderella watched them go. When they had disappeared from sight she began to cry.

Her godmother found her in tears and asked what was wrong.

'I'd like . . . I'd like . . .' She was crying so hard that she couldn't go on.

Her godmother, who was a fairy, said, 'You'd like to go to the ball, wouldn't you?'

'Oh dear, I would,' said Cinderella with a sigh.

'Well, be a good girl,' said her godmother, 'and you shall.'

She took Cinderella into her own room and said, 'Go into the garden and bring me a pumpkin.' Cinderella picked the best she could find and took it to her godmother, though she couldn't imagine how a pumpkin would help her to get to the ball.

Her godmother cut out the inside, leaving just the rind. Then she struck it with her wand, and immediately the pumpkin changed into a splendid golden coach.

Then she looked in the mouse-trap and found six mice, all alive. She told Cinderella to lift the gate of the trap, and as each mouse came out she tapped it with her wand and it turned into a thoroughbred horse. They made a team of six fine bays, with a touch of mouse.

The godmother couldn't think what to do about a coachman.

'I'll look in the rat-trap,' said Cinderella, 'and see if there's a rat. We could make him into a coachman.'

'A good idea,' said her godmother. 'Go and see.'

Cinderella brought her the rat-trap and there were three big rats in it. The fairy picked out one for his

53

luxuriant whiskers, and when she had tapped him with her wand he was changed into a stout coachman with a magnificent moustache. Then she said, 'Go into the garden, you'll find six lizards behind the watering-can. Bring them here.'

The moment Cinderella brought them her god-mother changed them into six footmen, who sprang up behind the coach in their dazzling liveries and stood there as if they had done nothing else all their lives.

Then the fairy said to Cinderella, 'Well, now you can go to the ball. Aren't you pleased?'

'Yes, but how can I go like this, in my ugly old clothes?'

Her godmother just touched her with her wand and at once her clothes turned into a ball-dress covered with jewels. Then the fairy gave her a pair of glass slippers, the prettiest in the world. Dressed in her finery, Cinderella got into the coach, but her god-mother warned her on no account to stay later than midnight, for if she remained a moment longer at the ball her coach would become a pumpkin again, her horse mice, her footmen lizards, and her clothes rags and tatters.

She promised that she would certainly leave before midnight and set off, almost beside herself with joy.

When she arrived, the servants told the prince that an unknown princess had just appeared, and he hurried to welcome her. He helped her out of the carriage and led her into the ballroom. At once there was complete silence; the dancers stopped dancing and the musicians stopped playing; everyone was spellbound by the loveliness of the unknown lady. A murmur ran round the room: 'How beautiful she is!' Even the king, elderly as he was, couldn't stop looking at her, and he said to the queen that it was years since he had seen anyone so beautiful and charming. All the ladies looked carefully at her clothes, making up their minds to have a dress made the very next day in the same style, if they could find such exquisite materials and such clever dressmakers.

The prince led her to the place of honour and then asked for the next dance. She danced so gracefully that the company admired her more than ever. A splendid supper was served, but the prince ate nothing; he could only gaze at her. She sat beside her sisters and showed them every attention. She even shared with them the oranges and lemons that the prince had given her, which surprised them greatly, for they didn't recognize her.

While they were talking, Cinderella heard the clock strike a quarter to twelve. At once she curtseyed to the company, and went away as fast as she could. As soon as she reached home, she went to find her godmother, and after thanking her, she said that she was very anxious to go to the ball again the next night, because the prince had invited her. As she was telling her godmother everything that had happened at the ball, the two stepsisters knocked at the door, and Cinderella went to open it.

'How late you are!' she said, yawning and rubbing her eyes, and stretching as if she had only just woken up, though in fact she had not felt at all sleepy since her sisters had left the house.

'If you'd come to the ball,' said one of them, 'you wouldn't have been bored. A beautiful princess was there, the most beautiful ever seen. She was extremely polite to us; she gave us oranges and lemons.'

Cinderella was delighted to hear this. She asked the princess's name, but they told her that no one knew and that the prince would give anything to learn who the lady was.

Cinderella smiled and said, 'She was very beautiful, then? Oh, how lucky you are! Why can't I see her? Oh, Miss Javotte, lend me your yellow dress, the one you wear every day.'

'Really,' said Miss Javotte, 'what an idea! Lend my dress to a grubby Cinders like you! I'd be crazy.'

Cinderella was expecting this refusal and was quite happy about it, for she would have been in a quandary if her sister had actually wanted to lend her a dress.

The next day the two sisters were at the ball, and Cinderella too, even more splendidly dressed than the first time. The prince was always at her side, and paid her endless compliments. She was very far from bored and quite forgot what her godmother had told her, so that she heard the first stroke of midnight when she had supposed that it was only eleven o'clock.

She sprang up and fled as lightly as a deer. The prince followed her, but he couldn't catch up with her. However, she lost one of her glass slippers and he picked it up very carefully.

Cinderella arrived home out of breath, without a coach, without footmen, in her old clothes; nothing remained of her splendour but one of her little slippers, the twin of the one she had lost.

The palace guards were asked if they had seen the princess leave, but they said they had seen no one except a ragged girl who looked more like a peasant than a great lady.

When the two sisters came home Cinderella asked if they had enjoyed themselves and if the beautiful lady had been there. They said yes, but that she had fled at the stroke of midnight, so fast that she had dropped one of her pretty little glass slippers, and the prince had picked it up and done nothing but look at it for the rest of the ball. They thought he must be madly in love with the beautiful lady it belonged to.

They were right, for a few days later the prince had it proclaimed, to the sound of a trumpet, that he would marry the lady whose foot the slipper fitted. The princesses tried it on first, then the duchesses, and then all the court ladies, but in vain. At length it was brought to the house of the sisters and they tried hard to force their feet into it, but without success. Cinderella was watching them and she recognized her slipper.

'Let me try,' she said.

Her sisters laughed scornfully, but the gentleman who had brought the slipper looked at her closely and saw that she was very beautiful. So he said that she was quite right, his orders were to offer the slipper to every girl. He made Cinderella sit down and when he held out the slipper her little foot slipped in as easily as if it had been made for her.

The sisters were amazed, but they were more astonished still when Cinderella took the other little slipper out of her pocket and put it on. Her godmother appeared and tapped her with her wand; and at once she was even more magnificently dressed than when she went to the ball.

Then the two sisters recognized her as the beautiful lady they had seen at the ball. They knelt before her and asked her forgiveness for treating her so badly. Cinderella kissed them and forgave them with all her heart, and begged them always to love her.

Then she was escorted to the prince in her grand new clothes. He found her lovelier than ever and a few days later they were married. Cinderella, who was as good as she was beautiful, took her sisters to live at the palace and married them on the same day to two great noblemen.

CHARLES PERRAULT

The Princess on the Pea

There was once a prince who wanted to marry a princess, a *truly real* princess. So off he went travelling all over the world looking for one, but there was always something that wasn't *quite* right. For although there were lots of princesses, the prince could never be absolutely certain whether they were *real* princesses or not; there was always something that didn't quite click. So back he came from his travels, very sad indeed, for he had so wanted to find a *real* princess.

One night there was a terrible storm – thunder and lightning and pouring rain – it was quite frightening. And in the middle of it all there was a violent knocking at the town gate and the old king himself went to open it. And there outside stood a princess. But goodness me! What a sight she was, what with all that wind and rain! Water ran down her hair and clothes, trickling in through the toes of her shoes and out again at her heels. But she insisted she was a *real* princess!

'We can soon find out about that!' thought the old queen, though she didn't actually say anything to the wet lady outside. She went up to the spare bedroom, removed all the bedclothes from the bed and put one pea on the bedstead. Then she got twenty mattresses, put them on top of the pea and then put a further twenty eiderdowns on top of the mattresses.

And in this bed the princess was to pass the night!

Next morning they asked her how she had slept.

'Oh shockingly!' replied the princess. 'I hardly slept a wink the whole night. I can't imagine what there was in the bed but it must have been something very hard because I'm black and blue all over. It was dreadful!'

Now they could see that she *was* a real princess because only a real princess would have felt the pea through twenty mattresses and twenty eiderdowns. No one except a real princess could be as tender-skinned as that.

So the prince married her, for now he knew for certain that she was a true princess. As for the pea, it was placed in a museum, and you can still see it there, unless someone has taken it away.

How about that for a real story!

HANS CHRISTIAN ANDERSEN

Aladdin and
the Wonderful Lamp

In the capital of the kingdom of China in ancient times there lived a poor tailor named Mustapha. He had a son called Aladdin, a good-for-nothing, ill-behaved, disobedient lad. Hard as his father tried to teach him his trade, he was forever idling away his time, playing in the streets with other ne'er-do-wells and stubbornly refusing to learn a thing. This behaviour caused poor Mustapha so much grief that he fell sick and died.

Aladdin's mother earned what little she could by spinning and selling cotton, with no help whatsoever from her son.

One day Aladdin, now a youth of fifteen, was wasting his time as usual with his vagabond companions, when a passing stranger approached him in the square and asked him his name.

'Is not your father Mustapha the tailor?' he asked.

'Yes,' replied Aladdin, 'but he is dead long since.'

The stranger threw his arms round Aladdin's neck and kissed him several times with tears in his eyes.

'Alas, my poor boy, your father was my beloved brother. I have been travelling these many years, and I arrived here hoping to meet my long-lost brother and see his dear face again. It is most grievous news that he has passed away. But it is a great comfort in my affliction that I can recognize his features in your face,

61

and it was no mere chance that I picked you out of the crowd.'

He gave Aladdin a handful of coins, and told him to go home to his mother and inform her that he would soon be coming to visit her.

'Yes, indeed,' said his mother on hearing the news. 'It is true that your father had a brother, but I thought he had died many years back.' But she now busied herself to prepare, as best she could, a meal for her visitor, who soon arrived laden with fruit and wines. After greeting her with a show of great emotion, he prostrated himself before the stool where his brother had sat and pressed his lips to it, exclaiming tearfully, 'Miserable am I not to have seen my brother before he died. I have travelled the wide world, and a longing seized me to return to the land of my birth and my kin. And now I learn that my brother, whom I loved as my life, is dead. Praise be to Allah that Aladdin, his son, is alive and well.'

Turning to Aladdin, he asked him what trade he plied. The boy looked down and his mother bewailed her son's idleness.

'This will not do,' said the uncle. 'I propose to set you up in a shop stocked with costly materials, where you will meet with rich merchants and people of rank and quality.' Aladdin's mother besought her son to make himself worthy of his uncle's generosity.

The following day he arranged for Aladdin to be arrayed in clothes befitting the most prosperous of merchants, and introduced him to people of wealth and importance, while his mother was overjoyed to behold him so grandly attired.

A few days later his uncle led Aladdin along a road leading out of the city and further and further from his home. As they approached the mountains he told amazing stories to divert the boy from wishing to return, and pointed out magnificent palaces and ornate gardens, each excelling the previous one in splendour and beauty.

'Let us rest a while,' he said at last, and they sat down by a fountain whose waters gushed from the jaws of a marble lion. His uncle spread before Aladdin a white cloth with a choice of luscious fruits and delicacies, and he ate his fill. Then they continued their journey till they reached two great mountains separated by a valley.

'We will go no further,' said the uncle. 'Pray gather some sticks, and I will show you such wonders as are unknown to mortal man.' He set light to the sticks and threw upon the flames a perfumed powder; then, swaying mysteriously from side to side, he intoned a spell. Immediately there arose a thick pall of smoke, and the earth opened up to reveal a large stone slab with a bronze ring sealed into its centre.

Aladdin took fright and was about to take to his heels, but his uncle struck him a blow that threw him to the ground. Poor Aladdin cried out piteously, 'What have I done to deserve such treatment?'

'I have my reasons,' shouted his uncle. 'I am your father's brother and you must obey me to the letter. Beneath this stone lies a hidden treasure which will make you richer than all the kings in the world. No one but you is allowed to raise this stone. Even I am forbidden to do so, nor may I place a foot inside the vault. This treasure is destined to be yours if you do exactly as I instruct you.'

Listening to all this, Aladdin forgot his uncle's brutality and asked what he must do.

'Seize hold of this bronze ring,' said his uncle, in a gentler tone, 'and by uttering the names of your father and grandfather you will be enabled to raise this stone with ease. You will then descend some steps leading to a door opening on to a vaulted area divided into three large rooms containing bronze vases brimming with silver and gold. But beware! Touch nothing – not even the walls – with your robe! That would mean your immediate death. Pass through these three rooms without pausing and then through a door into a garden filled with trees laden with the most extra-ordinary fruits. Walk straight on and thence up fifty steps on to a terrace, and there, in a niche, you will behold a lighted lamp. Extinguish the flame, pour out the oil and carefully tuck the lamp inside your robe next to your chest, and bring it straight back to me.' Then, taking a ring from one of his fingers, he placed it on one of Aladdin's, saying that it would protect him against all harm.

Aladdin descended to the foot of the steps and found the three rooms just as his uncle had described them. He passed through them with care, on into the garden and up the steps to the terrace. He took the lamp from the niche, emptied it of oil and tucked it into his robe. On the way back he noticed that the trees were laden with extraordinary fruits of every conceivable colour. The deepest red were, in reality, rubies; the green ones were emeralds, the violet amethysts, the yellow sapphires and the white ones pearls. And there were numerous others of equally dazzling and flawless perfection, but to poor, innocent Aladdin these priceless gems were nothing but glass baubles which he was tempted to pick simply because of their size and prettiness. He stuffed as many as he could into his pockets and down his shirt, and soon appeared at the entrance to the vault at the foot of the steps, where his uncle impatiently awaited him.

'Pray help me, Uncle,' called Aladdin, but his uncle shouted back, 'First give me the lamp!'

Aladdin had the lamp tangled up with the glassy fruits, and he refused to part with it until he was out of the cave. His uncle flew into a frightful rage and threw some scented powder on the fire, which was still burning. Scarcely had he uttered a magic incantation when the slab replaced itself and the vault was closed.

Certain it is that this man was *not* the brother of Mustapha the tailor, so he was no uncle to Aladdin. He was indeed from Africa, where he had practised magic diligently since his youth and had finally discovered the existence of a miraculous lamp in a subterranean cave in the heart of far-off China. Possession of this lamp would make him the most powerful man in the universe. However, although he alone knew where the lamp was, he was not permitted to enter the vault to seize it; he could receive it only from the hands of another, which was why he had chosen Aladdin to perform this task. Once the lamp was in his hands, his intention was to kill the boy and thus be rid of any witness. And now his great scheme had foundered and his only course was to return to Africa that same day. He assumed that Aladdin would perish, buried alive in utter darkness with no hope of escape. The boy cried out to his 'uncle' a thousand times – in vain. After two days of piteous crying and lamenting, with neither food nor drink, he raised his hands in prayer, appealing to the great God on high. With his hands thus clasped he unwittingly rubbed the ring which the magician had placed on his finger.

Immediately an enormous genie rose out of the earth and spoke these words: 'What is thy wish? I am ready to obey thee in all things, for I am the slave of the ring.' At any other time Aladdin would have remained speechless with fear, but now, thinking only of his danger, he replied without hesitation, 'Whoever you may be, deliver me from this place.' No sooner were the words spoken than the earth opened and he found himself outside the vault.

At first his eyes could not bear the light, but he gradually discerned the path along which his false uncle had led him, and finally he arrived in the town and dragged himself to his home, where he fell in a faint on the doorstep. His mother had given him up for dead and her joy knew no bounds.

When he came to, his mother revived him with food and drink, and Aladdin told her how the magician had deceived him, and showed her the lamp and the glassy fruits he had picked in the garden. Like her son she was ignorant of the value of these priceless gems, and Aladdin placed them under some cushions on the sofa.

Next day Aladdin was still hungry, but his mother told him, 'Alas, I have no more food. I shall sell the cotton I have spun and fetch you something back with what little money I can make.'

'No, Mother,' said Aladdin, 'keep your cotton and sell the lamp instead.'

The lamp being very dirty, Aladdin's mother began to rub and clean it so that it might fetch a little more money. Hardly had she given the first rub when a hideous giant of a genie rose up and in a voice of thunder said, 'What wouldst thou with me? I am the slave of the lamp, ready to obey thee in all things.' The woman fell into a faint, but Aladdin, who had already seen a similar apparition, took hold of the lamp and said firmly, 'Bring me food, I am hungry.'

Instantly the genie disappeared, to reappear just as rapidly with a tray of solid gold upon his head, on which there were twelve silver vessels full of the most excellent meats, six great loaves of bread, two bottles of the finest wine and two silver goblets. Then he vanished. When Aladdin's mother recovered she asked in amazement how such a feast had appeared.

'Do not fear, Mother,' said Aladdin. 'Let us eat. This genie is the genie of the lamp. The genie in the cave who saved my life was the genie of the ring – this ring on my finger.' His mother begged him to sell the lamp for fear that they might die through touching the cursed thing. 'We must have no truck with genies,' she cried. But Aladdin soothed her, saying, 'I should certainly beware of selling a lamp which could prove so useful to us. See what it has provided us with. It is a miraculous lamp, and it is not without reason that my false and wicked uncle undertook such a long and arduous journey to gain possession of it.'

The following day Aladdin hid one of the silver dishes under his clothes, went into the town and sold it to a merchant for a mere gold coin. With this he bought provisions and gave what was left of the money to his mother. He then sold all the dishes, one after the other, for the same price, until none was left. The solid gold tray, being ten times heavier than each dish, fetched ten gold pieces.

When they had used up all the gold coins, Aladdin again rubbed the lamp and the genie obliged with the same wondrous feast in silver dishes on a gold tray. This time, however, Aladdin took his wares to a more honest merchant, who gave him seventy-two gold pieces for each dish and tenfold that number for the tray. He now had an almost inexhaustible source of money, but they continued to live in their humble dwelling and his mother spent no more on her clothes than she received for the cotton she spun. In this fashion they lived for many years, using the lamp prudently whenever it was necessary.

At length Aladdin began frequenting the company of people of importance whom he encountered in shops and markets, and he soon became wiser in the ways of the world. He learned the true value of the precious gems which he had previously taken to be transparent glass fruits and realized that he was in possession of priceless treasures. This, however, he revealed to no one.

One day he heard a proclamation that all shops, doors and shutters were to be closed and everyone was to stay indoors until the Princess Badroulboud-our, the Sultan's daughter, had passed on her way to bathe and returned to the palace. Aladdin was seized with a desire to behold her face. He peeped through the shutters as she passed, but he was not satisfied, for she wore a veil. So he hid behind the outer door of the bathing chamber, where he could see her through a cleft in the door without himself being seen. When he saw the unveiled face of the princess his heart was drawn like a magnet to her beauty, for until that moment he had never looked at the face of an unveiled woman except his mother's. The princess's charm and dignity left him in a state of speechless ecstasy. He returned home as one in a dream, and it was a long time before his mother could learn the cause of his melancholy silence.

After persistent questioning he finally spoke and

told his mother how he had come to see the princess. And then he burst out with these words: 'I have fallen so madly in love with her that I am unable to describe my feelings to you, and as my ardour increases with each passing moment I have resolved to ask the Sultan to grant me her hand in marriage.' These last words brought a loud burst of laughter from his mother.

'My son,' she said, 'you must have taken leave of your senses to think of such things.'

'I can assure you, Mother,' replied Aladdin, 'that I am in full control of my mind and, Mother, it will be through you that I shall achieve my aim. It is a favour I beg of you which you must fulfil unless you wish to see me die.'

The good woman looked at her son in blank amazement.

'I am your mother,' she said, 'who brought you into this world, and there is no reasonable thing I would not readily do for you. But have you forgotten that you are the son of a humble tailor and that your mother is of the lowliest birth?'

'I confess, Mother, I may seem overbold, but I have now learned the priceless value of the coloured glass fruits which I brought you back from the subterranean cave. A present of this rarity could not but be agreeable to the Sultan.' When Aladdin arranged the jewelled stones in a porcelain dish, both mother and son were dazzled by their brilliant beauty. She could now see that nothing on earth would divert Aladdin from his aim, and he prevailed upon her to proceed to the Sultan's palace on his behalf.

The next morning she wrapped the porcelain dish in a double linen cloth and made her way to the palace. Following the Grand Vizier and all his attendants, she entered the audience chamber. Petitioners were summoned, one after the other, to the presence of the Sultan, but Aladdin's mother did not dare to step forward and declare her mission in the presence of such powerful officers of the court. So she returned home without having spoken a word. For six days she went to the palace without addressing the Sultan and might have gone for a hundred more days had not the Sultan noticed her. He said to the Grand Vizier, 'I have observed that woman for several days. She comes each day carrying something wrapped in a cloth and leaves each time without saying a word. If she comes again, do not fail to bring her before me.'

The next day, therefore, the Grand Vizier himself conducted Aladdin's mother into the Sultan's presence. She prostrated herself on the carpet of the steps at the foot of his throne, where she remained until the Sultan commanded her to rise.

'I have watched you many days,' he said. 'Tell me, my good woman, what is your business here?' She prostrated herself a second time and on rising she said, 'Sublime monarch of the universe, I beseech you to forgive the boldness of the request which I, the lowliest of your subjects, am about to make.'

'Rest assured,' replied the Sultan, 'no harm will come to you. Speak freely.'

She then told him of Aladdin's violent passion for the princess and how she had tried in vain to divert him from such an insane course, but that he had threatened to kill himself if she refused to speak to the Sultan and to ask him, on her son's behalf, for his daughter's hand in marriage. The monarch then asked her what she had brought wrapped in the linen cloth. She uncovered the porcelain bowl. The Sultan's amazement and admiration at the sight of those enormous precious stones, dazzling and flawless, were beyond description. He remained silent for some moments, then turning to his Grand Vizier, he asked, 'Is not this a gift worthy of my daughter and should I hesitate to give my child in marriage to the man who values her at such a price and who now seeks her hand?' The Grand Vizier became strangely agitated, for the Sultan had only recently hinted his intention of giving the princess in marriage to his own son.

'One cannot dispute,' he replied after a pause, 'that this gift is worthy of the princess, but I beg Your Majesty to reflect and grant me three months before you make your final decision. I am certain that before that time is over my son will be in a position to offer an even more magnificent gift than that of this unknown suitor.' The Sultan granted his request and turning to Aladdin's mother he said, 'Return to your home, my good lady, and tell your son that I agree to the proposal that you have made on his behalf, but I cannot allow my daughter to be married until suitable royal apartments have been prepared for her. Pray return in three months' time.'

Overjoyed by such a response, Aladdin's mother hurried to tell her son every detail of her audience with the Sultan and of his request for a delay of three months. Aladdin's happiness knew no bounds, and he now began to count not only the weeks and days but even the hours and minutes of the months of waiting.

After eight weeks had passed Aladdin's mother went into the town to purchase oil for the lamp. She noticed that the whole place was full of excitement and rejoicing, and she asked the oil merchant the meaning of it all.

'Where do you come from, my good woman?' he asked her in surprise. 'Are you not aware that the son of the Grand Vizier is this very night to be wedded to the Princess Badroulboudour?'

Aladdin's mother hurried home. 'All is lost, my son,' she said. 'The Sultan has forgotten his promise.' Aladdin was thunderstruck at the news, but remembering the lamp he said, 'Mother, I can wager that the Grand Vizier's son will not be as happy tonight as he thinks he is going to be.'

He then rubbed the lamp and the genie appeared, uttering his usual words.

'Genie,' said Aladdin, 'the Princess Badroulboudour was promised to me in marriage by the Sultan himself, but he has failed to keep that promise. Tonight she is to be wedded to the Grand Vizier's son. What I now ask of you is this: as soon as the groom and his bride are abed, bring them both here to my house *in their bed*.'

'Master,' replied the genie, 'to hear is to obey.' He then vanished, and by nightfall he was back with the bride and groom in their marriage bed. On Aladdin's command he removed the bridegroom from the bed and shut him up in a dark and extremely cold closet. 'Guard him so that he is unable even to stir,' added Aladdin. The genie did as he was bidden: by simply blowing upon the bridegroom he rendered him unable to move, and there he had to remain, shivering with fear, in utter misery.

'Fear nothing,' said Aladdin to the princess, 'you are here in perfect safety. I shall never overstep the bounds of the deep respect I have for you. I did not force you here to offer you any offence, but to prevent an unjust rival from becoming your husband when the

Sultan had promised you would be my bride. And now, most adored and honoured princess, sleep in peace till morning, when you will be safely returned to your father's palace.'

Early next day the genie appeared at the appointed hour, and fetched the shivering bridegroom from the closet, placed him in the bed and transported the couple to the palace. Through the course of all these happenings the genie had made himself visible neither to the Vizier's son nor to the princess, for fear of frightening them.

In the morning the Sultan came to greet his daughter, but the Grand Vizier's son, chilled to the marrow as a result of the way he had spent the night in the ice-cold closet, arose immediately he heard the door open and sped into his dressing-room.

The Sultan saw that his daughter was in a state of great distress. But no words came from her lips, so he sent her mother to her. 'Tell me, child,' she began, 'why do you not respond to your father's greeting?'

The princess sighed deeply. 'Pardon me, Mother,' she replied, sobbing, 'if I have been lacking in the proper respect I owe to you and to my father.' And then she recounted in vivid detail all that had happened during the night.

The Sultana listened without believing a word, and told her not to repeat to her father or anyone else what she had just related to her. 'People will certainly think that you have lost your senses,' she concluded.

The Vizier's son was too much abashed to talk about his own mishap, but the following night the same strange misadventures were repeated. The unhappy princess could not face angering her father a second time.

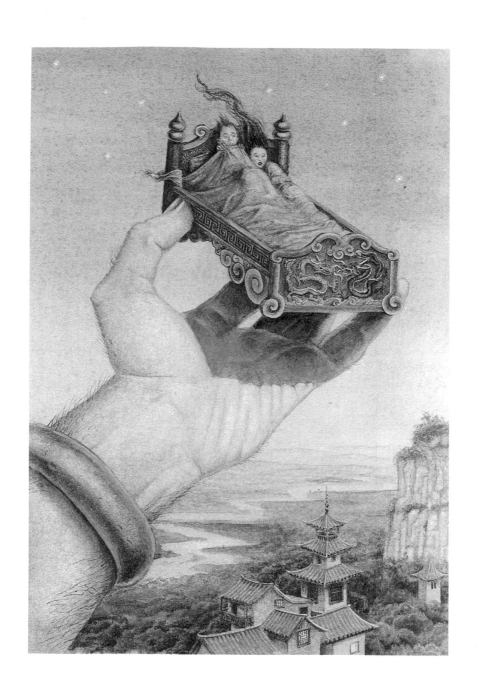

'My beloved Sire,' she cried finally, breaking her embarrassed silence, 'I know you will forgive me when you have heard what took place these last two nights.'

The Sultan summoned his Grand Vizier and ordered him to ask his son to confirm his daughter's account of the two nights' happenings. Whereupon the young man confessed that the princess's account was true, adding that those two nights were the most painful he had ever spent, and that despite his great love for the princess and the glory and honour of a union with the royal house, he would prefer to die rather than undergo such humiliation again. 'I beg you, revered Father,' he concluded, 'to beseech the Sultan to declare our marriage null and void.'

The Grand Vizier sadly informed the Sultan of all this and begged him to allow his son to retire from the palace, and the Sultan granted his plea.

And now three months had passed, and Aladdin sent his mother to remind the monarch of his promise. She accordingly made her way to the palace and presented herself as before. The Sultan recognized her and recalled her request; she was summoned to the foot of the throne, where she prostrated herself, saying, 'The three months have elapsed, Your Majesty, and I come, on behalf of Aladdin, my son, to renew the petition I made to you.'

Embarrassing though the Sultan found it to go back on his word, he felt little inclined to give his daughter in marriage to some unknown and probably unsuitable youth, whose mother appeared before him in such a humble dress. He consulted his Grand Vizier, who told him that there was an easy way out of the difficulty. 'Your Majesty,' he advised, 'must set such an impossibly high price on the princess that whatever Aladdin's wealth it will be insufficient to maintain her at the level you demand.'

Then the Sultan, turning to Aladdin's mother, said, 'My good woman, a monarch must indeed honour his promise and I will not forget mine. But in order to show the princess the honour she deserves, he must first send here forty golden bowls filled with precious stones, such as you have shown me, borne by forty black slaves escorted by forty white slaves, each one perfectly proportioned and dressed with suitable magnificence. Go now, good lady. I shall await your reply.'

After prostrating herself once more, Aladdin's mother withdrew, believing that her son's hopes had finally been thwarted. She gave him a detailed account of the Sultan's demands, adding, 'I suspect he will have to wait a long time for your reply.'

'Not as long as you may think, Mother,' answered Aladdin. 'His Majesty deludes himself if he believes he can put me off with his exorbitant demands. But I am content. It is but little compared with what I *could* do.'

Aladdin now rubbed his lamp and the genie appeared. After being provided with every detail of the Sultan's requirements he disappeared, only to reappear within seconds, accompanied by eighty slaves. Each of the black slaves bore a golden bowl upon his head brimful with the choicest pearls, rubies, diamonds and emeralds. A cloth of ultra-fine linen embossed with silver and gold embroidery covered each bowl. The astonishment of Aladdin's mother on beholding this blinding display of wealth was beyond words, but Aladdin, without delay, sent her off to the Sultan with this amazing dowry. People stopped to gape in wonderment as the procession passed through the streets, the apparel of the slaves and their proud bearing presenting a spectacle beyond the experience of even the most experienced traveller. At the palace gates the slave leading the cortège was taken to be a king and the porters hurried to bow low and kiss the hem of his garment. 'We are but slaves,' they were told. 'Our master himself will appear in due course.' The magnificence and dazzling splendour of the gift-bearers outshone anything even the Sultan's courtiers could boast. Forming a semi-circle round the throne, the slaves knelt before the Sultan, and each of the forty placed his golden bowl on the carpet, kissing the ground as he did so. Aladdin's mother, having pros-trated herself before the monarch, thus addressed him: 'My son is well aware that his gifts are over-shadowed by the peerless beauty of the princess, but he nevertheless begs you to consider them acceptable, inasmuch as he has made every effort to conform to your wishes and to the conditions you have laid down.'

The Sultan, speechless with admiration, scarcely heeded her words. He did not even pause to inquire about Aladdin's other qualities. 'My dear lady,' he said, 'tell your son I am waiting to receive him with open arms.'

She thanked him profusely, and hastened to report to Aladdin that the Sultan was eagerly awaiting him to conclude the marriage settlement. Aladdin summoned the genie and requested him to prepare a perfumed bath, and clothing of matchless splendour, and to have ready a horse with gold-emblazoned trappings. Not forgetting his mother, he ordered that she too was to be arrayed in suitable apparel and provided with a retinue of male and female slaves.

77

Aladdin now mounted his horse and set off at the head of his procession, bearing himself like a prince. He was no longer recognizable to his one-time vagabond playmates.

Arriving at the palace, he was embraced by the Sultan, who led him, to a fanfare of trumpets, into a great hall where a banquet had been prepared, intended to celebrate the marriage that very day. Aladdin, however, requested a brief delay in order that he might have a palace erected fit for a princess of such inestimable qualities.

Once again he summoned the genie of the lamp and ordered him to build a palace of the finest white marble directly opposite that of the Sultan, the marble to be inlaid with precious stones of the most varied colours, including jasper, porphyry, agate and lapis lazuli. Its centrepiece was to be a great hall topped with a lofty dome supported by columns of silver and gold. In this hall there were to be twenty-four windows, twenty-three of which were to be framed with the rarest and largest diamonds, rubies and emeralds, but the twenty-fourth was to be left unframed. Elaborate gardens with ornate fountains would surround the palace; outhouses with stables were to be erected at a suitable distance from the palace gardens, and a fleet of horses with grooms, and female slaves for the kitchens were to be supplied at the genie's discretion. Finally a secret treasure-house to store unlimited gold and silver was to be erected.

By the next morning Aladdin's orders had been executed down to the very last detail. He then requested a velvet carpet to be laid down, extending from the Sultan's palace to his own.

Aladdin's mother, escorted by her impressive

78

retinue of women slaves, was followed by her son on his superb charger. He had left his home for ever, but, of course, he had taken with him his invaluable lamp. The triumphant sound of drums, trumpets and cymbals accompanied Aladdin as he neared the palace.

The princess received Aladdin's mother with the greatest honour. After the marriage had been celebrated, the princess embraced her father and walked along the velvet carpet to her new home, where she was greeted at the palace entrance by her husband. He apologized for the unhappiness he had caused her in his efforts to win her, and she was charmed with him, and full of happiness. Aladdin led her into the central hall, where a sumptuous banquet had been prepared, and they supped to the accompaniment of joyous music and the performances of acrobats and dancers.

The next morning Aladdin called on the Sultan to invite him to inspect his palace. On entering the hall of the twenty-four windows studded with diamonds, emeralds and rubies, the monarch exclaimed, 'Surely this must be the wonder of the world.' But he was surprised to find that one window had been left unframed and asked Aladdin whether this was an accident or due to lack of time. 'It is neither, Your Majesty,' replied Aladdin. 'It was my humble desire that you, Your Majesty, should grant me the honour of seeing to its completion yourself.'

'That favour will I gladly perform,' replied the Sultan graciously, and forthwith he ordered the finest craftsmen to carry out the task. However, after many months of effort they came to him and shamefacedly admitted that nowhere had they been able to find jewels comparable in rarity and beauty to those adorning the other twenty-three windows. Aladdin, of course, had known that this would happen, and he asked the Sultan's permission to complete the last frame himself. He called on the genie to perform the work, and then received the Sultan and with great deference conducted him to the finished window. The monarch was speechless with admiration at its perfect likeness to the other windows.

'What manner of man are you?' he asked at last. 'You can have no peer in the entire world.'

Aladdin often rode through the town accompanied by his slaves, who threw handfuls of gold into the crowd. Never did a beggar present himself at the palace without receiving generous alms. Aladdin won all hearts by his grace and gentle bearing, and helped to suppress a rebellion against the Sultan, showing great valour in leading the army.

Several years passed in this way, but far off in Africa the magician now discovered by the use of his magic arts that Aladdin, who, he thought, had perished miserably in the cave, was married to the princess and living in a state of unparalleled splendour. He went purple with rage and vowed that this wretched son of a tailor should not enjoy for much longer the fruits of his magic lamp.

The very next day he set out, and travelled night and day until he reached the capital of China. As he walked about the town he listened to the people talking, and heard mention of Aladdin and his amazing palace. When he questioned a passer-by about it, the man exclaimed, 'You must see it for yourself, it is not to be missed,' and conducted him to it.

Now the magician's one thought was how to get possession of the lamp and bring about Aladdin's downfall. He learned that Aladdin was away on a hunting party, and his next move was to buy a dozen copper lamps. Putting them in a basket, he wended his way slowly towards the palace, crying, 'New lamps for old! New lamps for old!' Onlookers thought he was mad, but finally the princess herself heard him and dispatched a slave to find out the meaning of this strange pedlar's cries. The slave returned laughing hugely. 'He has dozens of shining new lamps,' she reported, 'which he is ready to exchange for any old ones.' And then she added, 'You could test it for yourself if you wished, Your Highness, by offering him your old lamp standing over there in the cornice.' The princess, ignorant of its value, sent out another slave with Aladdin's precious lamp and an exchange was soon made. The magician immediately stopped advertising his wares and hastened out of town.

He waited till nightfall and then rubbed the lamp. The genie appeared, and the magician commanded him to transport him to his home in Africa, together with the palace and everything and every person within it.

Next morning the Sultan went to his window to enjoy, as usual, the pleasure of looking at Aladdin's palace. He was dumbfounded and for many long minutes remained transfixed, hoping against hope that the palace would reappear. Finally he summoned the Grand Vizier, whose astonishment was no less than the Sultan's but who insisted that he had always believed that Aladdin worked through dark magic powers. In an outburst of terrifying fury the Sultan roared, 'Fetch me that scoundrel, that impostor, that I may watch him die with my own eyes.' The palace guards, on receiving the order, surrounded Aladdin as

he approached on horseback, chained him and
dragged him back to the Sultan like an ordinary crimi-
nal. The monarch ordered his immediate execution;
Aladdin's eyes were bound with a cloth and the executioner was about to strike when a crowd of people
scaled the palace walls with a tremendous outcry to
rescue their hero. They seemed so threatening that the
Sultan ordered the executioner to stay his hand, and
issued a proclamation that Aladdin was to be freed
and pardoned.

Aladdin now begged the Sultan to tell him what
crime he had committed.

'Come and look through my window,' said the monarch grimly. 'Tell me, pray, where your palace is and
what has happened to my daughter, who is dearer to
me than my life. You *must* find her, or you will die.'

Aladdin tried to reassure the Sultan that he had had
no part in all this and begged to be allowed forty days
in which to find her. 'Sire,' he pleaded, 'if, at the end
of that time, I have not recovered your daughter, my
wife, I will place my head at the foot of your throne for
you to dispose of at your will.' His plea was granted
and Aladdin departed in a state of confusion and
despair.

For three whole days he wandered from door to
door inquiring if anyone knew what had happened to
his palace. At last he found himself in the countryside,
and he paused to rest by the bank of a river. In a
moment of utter dejection he was about to throw himself in when he paused to murmur a prayer. Clasping
his hands in reverence, he unwittingly rubbed the
ring, which was still on his finger. Immediately the
genie who had saved him from the subterranean cave
appeared.

'What wouldst thou have?' asked the spirit. 'I am the slave of the ring and am ready to obey thee.'

Aladdin begged the genie to save his life a second time by bringing back his palace and his princess.

'This is not in my power,' said the genie. 'You must address yourself to the slave of the lamp.'

'Then,' said Aladdin, 'I command you, the slave of the ring, to transport me to wherever my palace is and to set me down beneath my beloved wife's apartment.'

This was no sooner said than Aladdin found himself outside his palace in Africa, beneath the princess's window, where he fell asleep from sheer exhaustion. When he was awakened by the singing of birds, he slowly began to understand that all his misfortunes were due to the loss of his lamp, and he blamed himself bitterly for his carelessness.

Now the princess arose earlier that morning than she had done on any morning since she had been carried off by the magician. She had been forced to endure his company once a day, but she had been so cold and aloof that he had not dared to prolong his stay with her. She happened to look out of the window and could scarcely believe her eyes when she beheld Aladdin below. She beckoned him towards a secret door, and it is impossible to describe their joy as they tearfully embraced. Then he begged her:

'For all our sakes, tell me what became of the old lamp which I left in the cornice in the hall of the twenty-four windows.'

'Alas, beloved husband,' she cried, 'I have not ceased to grieve since I was spirited away here, knowing that it was I who caused our misfortune when I gave away the lamp.' She then told Aladdin of the cunning whereby the magician had procured it.

'Do not blame yourself,' said Aladdin. 'It is I who should have taken greater care. But tell me only where he keeps the lamp.'

'Alas,' replied the princess, 'he carries it about with him close to his heart. Daily he visits me, trying to persuade me to accept him as a husband in place of you. But now that you are here, dear husband, my anxieties are over.'

'Princess,' said Aladdin, 'I have devised a plan that will deliver us from this evil villain for ever, but you must follow my instructions in every detail.' He then told her to put on her most lavishly beautiful dress and jewels and to greet the magician with the warmest welcome on his next visit. 'Tell him you are making every effort to forget me, and invite him to sup and drink with you. You will put into his wine a special powder which I shall give you before he arrives, and you will direct your slave-in-waiting to place the goblet of wine containing the powder before *you*. And then, dear wife, you will exchange goblets with the villain, describing such an exchange as a compliment which he will surely be unable to refuse. As soon as he has partaken of the wine you will see him fall to the ground.'

Despite her reluctance even to pretend to welcome the evil man, the princess undertook to follow the instructions carefully.

She arrayed herself in her most sumptuous garments, her necklace, head-dress and girdle studded with the most precious stones. Her mirror told her that she was now more beautiful than ever, and when the magician arrived at his usual hour she received him with unexpected warmth and bade him accept the seat of honour at the table, which was prepared as if for a great banquet.

'I have pondered,' she told him, 'on what you have told me about Aladdin's deceit in robbing you of your lamp and I do not doubt that the Sultan, my father, has meted out to him the punishment he deserves. Tonight, therefore, I wish to rejoice and forget all sorrows. Now let us drink and exchange goblets in accordance with the custom between lovers.'

The magician, who had greedily drunk in every word that she had spoken, was now only too eager to obey. They exchanged goblets and no sooner had he drained his cup than his eyes began to rotate and he fell senseless to the ground.

At this point Aladdin came into the room, and the princess embraced him with tears of joy and relief. Removing the lamp from the magician's vest, he rubbed it, and when the genie appeared he gave instructions that he with his princess should be transported, in the palace, to the very spot where it had stood before the magician had done his mischief. This the genie performed by simply waving his hands twice and lo, there they were, back in China in their palace, exactly as before.

The Sultan, in the meantime, had been inconsolable, mourning his lost daughter day and night. As he looked gloomily through his window, expecting to see only the empty void, he thought that what now met his gaze must surely be a mirage. Imagine his joy when he realized that it was in very truth Aladdin's palace. He set off post-haste and Aladdin, foreseeing that this would happen, stood at the foot of the staircase to greet the monarch. 'Let me embrace my daughter before I say a word to you,' said the breathless Sultan.

The princess told her father that the pain of being snatched from him had been her chief suffering, but her delight at being rescued by her dear husband was unimaginable. Aladdin related the whole extraordinary story, and then, to confirm the truth of it, he conducted the Sultan to the chamber where the magician's corpse still lay, for, of course, it had been transported with the palace from Africa.

Thus Aladdin escaped with his life a second time, his mortal struggle with the evil magician had come to a happy conclusion, and he and the Princess Badroulboudour lived in peace and happiness.

from THE ARABIAN NIGHTS

Rapunzel

There once lived a man and his wife who had long wished, but wished in vain, to have a child. But after a very long time indeed, the woman really began to hope that the loving God would grant their wish.

At the back of their house these people had a small window, through which there was a view into a splendid garden filled with the most beautiful flowers and herbs. However, it was enclosed by a high wall, and no one dared to go inside it, because it belonged to a powerful witch who was dreaded by everyone.

One day, when the woman was standing by this window looking down into the garden, she saw a flower-bed adorned with the prettiest rapunzel plants you've ever seen. They looked so fresh and green that she felt a great craving to eat some of them. This longing grew more urgent from day to day, and when she realized she could never have them, she began to feel quite poorly and looked pale and miserable. Her husband took fright and asked her, 'What ails you, dear wife?'

'Ah!' she replied. 'If I do not get any rapunzel to eat from the garden behind our house, I shall surely die.'

The man, who loved her very much, thought, 'Sooner than allow my wife to die, I must fetch her some of the rapunzel whatever the cost.'

In the evening dusk he climbed over the wall into

the witch's garden, hastily snatched a handful of rapunzel plants and brought them back to his wife. She
immediately made a salad of them and ate it greedily.
But it tasted so good that the next day she had a
threefold yearning for more rapunzel, and if she were
to have peace of mind her husband must once more
climb into the garden. So after waiting for the evening
twilight he once again clambered over the wall. But
this time he had a terrible fright, for there was the
witch facing him.

'How dare you climb into my garden and steal my
rapunzel like any common thief?' she shrieked. 'You
will pay for this.'

'Oh, dear lady,' said the man, 'I beg you, have
mercy on me. I know I had no right to your rapunzel. I
did this only because I was forced to. My wife had
caught sight of your rapunzel through our window
and she felt so powerful a longing for it that she would
have died if she had not eaten some of it.'

Then the witch became less angry and said to him,
'Let it be as you say. I will permit you to take as much
rapunzel as you wish, but on one condition: you must
promise to hand over to me the child that your wife
will bring into the world. All will go well for the child,
and I shall care for it as though I were its own mother.'

The man was so terrified, and so anxious about his
wife, that he promised everything, and when the
woman gave birth to a baby the witch appeared immediately. She named the child Rapunzel and took it
away with her.

Rapunzel was the most beautiful child under the
sun. When she was twelve years of age the witch shut
her away in the heart of the forest in a tower which
had neither stairs nor door but only one tiny window

88

right at the very top. Whenever the witch wished to get into it she would stand below the tower and call out:

> *Rapunzel, Rapunzel, let down your hair*
> *That I may climb without a stair.*

Rapunzel had the most magnificent long hair, as fine as spun gold. When she heard the witch's voice she would untie her tresses and wind them round the window-hooks. Then her hair would fall twenty ells down to where the witch was standing, and she would climb up on it.

After a few years had passed it happened that the king's son was riding through the forest and came past the tower. Then he heard a song which he found so entrancing that he stood still and listened. It was Rapunzel, who used to while away her loneliness by letting her sweet voice resound through the air. The king's son wanted to climb up to her, and looked for a door to the tower, but there was none to be found. He rode back home, but the singing had stirred his heart so deeply that after that he rode every day into the forest and listened to it. One day, as he stood behind a tree, he saw the witch appear and heard her calling:

> *Rapunzel, Rapunzel, let down your hair*
> *That I may climb without a stair.*

At which Rapunzel let down her braids of hair, and the witch used them to climb up.

'Is that perhaps the ladder,' thought the prince, 'by which one climbs up? Then I too will try my luck.'

And the next day, as it drew near to dusk, he went to the tower and called:

Rapunzel, Rapunzel, let down your hair
That I may climb without a stair.

Immediately the tresses came falling down and the king's son climbed up.

At first Rapunzel was much frightened when a man, such as her eyes had never seen, came into her room. But the prince talked to her in such a friendly way and told her that his heart had been so deeply touched by her captivity that he had been left with no peace of mind and he felt he *must* see her. Then Rapunzel lost all her fears, and when he asked her if she would accept him as her husband and she saw that he was young and handsome, she thought, 'He will be kinder to me than the old dame.' So she said yes and placed her hand in his.

'I would gladly go with you,' she said, 'but I do not know how *I* can get down. When you come to see me, bring with you each time a skein of silk, and I shall weave a silken ladder. When it is ready I will climb down on it and you can take me away with you on your horse.' They arranged that until that time he would visit her every evening, for the old crone, Dame Gothel, used to come during the daytime. The witch noticed nothing of all this until one day Rapunzel forgot herself and said to her, 'Tell me, Dame Gothel, how is it that you are so much heavier to bring up here than the young prince? He was up here in a flash.'

'Ah! What is this I hear, you wicked child!' shrieked the old witch in a fury. 'What is this I hear! I thought I had cut you off from the whole world and yet you have deceived me!' In the frenzy of her rage she caught hold of Rapunzel's glorious hair, wound it twice round her left hand, seized the scissors with her right hand, and snip, snap, the tresses were cut off and lay pitifully on the floor. And she was so hard-hearted that she took poor Rapunzel into a deserted wasteland and left her there.

On the same day the witch fastened the shorn tresses to the hook of the window, and when the king's son arrived and called out:

Rapunzel, Rapunzel, let down your hair,

the witch herself let the hair down. The king's son climbed up, but what he found when he reached the top was not his beloved Rapunzel but the wicked crone, who looked at him with evil and venomous eyes.

'Aha!' she cried out with a sneer, 'you've come to fetch your wife, but the beautiful bird is no longer in her nest. No longer does she sing. The cat has seized her and it is ready to scratch your eyes out, too! Rapunzel is lost to you; never again will you set eyes on her.'

The prince was beside himself with grief, and in despair he leapt down from the tower. He escaped with his life, but the thorns into which he fell pierced his eyes and left him blind. Then he wandered, sightless, around the forest, ate only roots and berries and did nothing but weep and bemoan the loss of his beloved wife.

And so for some years he roamed about in utter misery, until at last he came to the deserted wasteland where Rapunzel, with her twins, a girl and a boy who had been born to her, lived in wretchedness. There he heard a voice which sounded familiar. He walked towards it, and as he drew nearer Rapunzel recognized him and fell on his neck and wept. Two of her tears wetted his eyes, which once again became clear so that he could see as he did before. He took Rapunzel and the little twins to his kingdom, where he was received with great joy, and they all lived happily ever after.

THE BROTHERS GRIMM

Baba Yaga,
the Bony-legged, the Witch

There was once an old man whose wife had died. He lived with his little daughter, and they were happy enough till he took it into his head to take to himself another wife. From that moment on all the joy went out of the little girl's life. Gone were the carefree days she had spent with her father, gone were the great helpings of delicious buttered bread and gooseberry jam which her father lovingly prepared for her, and gone, too, were the long, exciting rambles with her father in the woods.

For this new stepmother was truly the wickedest woman that ever lived. She scolded the little girl for this and punished her for that, and whenever the old man was out she made her do all the hard work. And she never stopped grumbling at her – from morning till night.

One day, as the three of them sat down to eat, she complained that the girl had been disobedient. 'She's not fit to sit at our table,' she said. 'Now out with you!' she suddenly shouted, pushing the child out of doors. 'Go and eat by yourself in the woodshed,' and she threw a few crusts of bread after her, which was all she gave her for her dinner.

The poor girl crept into a corner of the shed and stayed there all huddled up, sobbing her heart out. Suddenly she heard a tapping at the window. It was a nightingale, signalling to be let in. She opened the window and in he hopped, putting his head to one side and chirruping as a sign that he had something to say to her. She smiled through her tears at his perky little face; she was only too happy to have someone to talk to. She no longer felt all alone.

The nightingale spoke. 'I know why you're crying, little girl,' he said, 'but you won't feel lonely any more. I'm here to help you. I know all about that wicked stepmother of yours. I even know that she is a sister to the witch Baba Yaga, the bony-legged, who has iron teeth. Yes, Baba Yaga, who lives in the hut which moves about on hens' legs.'

The little girl shuddered and went pale with fear.

'Don't be afraid,' said the little bird. 'Your step-mother will one day send you to Baba Yaga, but this I promise, and promise with all my heart: you will come through whatever trouble you may find yourself in, because you have a kind heart and I shall tell you what you must do.'

The little girl felt happier after this and bravely managed a friendly smile for her new companion, and she shared a few crumbs of bread with him to show her gratitude.

The very next day it all happened. The stepmother said to the little girl, 'Today you must go to Baba Yaga, my sister, to fetch a needle and thread for me to mend a shirt.'

'Oh, please don't send me to Baba Yaga,' pleaded the girl. 'I know where to find a needle here in the house.'

'Hold your tongue and do as you're told,' said the stepmother. 'Go through the woods till you come to the fallen oak tree deep in the forest.' She gripped the poor girl's nose and gave it a sharp pinch. 'You can feel that, can't you?' she said roughly. 'So follow your nose and turn right when you get to the fallen oak tree, and you'll soon find Baba Yaga's hut. That's your dinner.' And she threw the girl a small bundle.

Now the little girl couldn't get back to the shed to tell her friend, so she ran through the forest as fast as her legs could carry her. But when she got to the fallen oak tree she began to think about the task which lay ahead and how she would carry it out. She thought she ought to eat something to give her a bit of courage, but when she sat down on the fallen oak tree and opened the bundle she couldn't believe her eyes. Nothing but stones were tied up in it. That is what the wicked woman had given her for her dinner. She emptied them on to the ground, and just missed hitting the head of her unexpected visitor, her new friend, the nightingale, who had hopped out from behind the tree. The bird saw the hot angry tears rolling down her cheeks and said, 'Look again, my friend, and see what you can see.' The little girl looked down and saw that the stones had changed into bread and butter and gooseberry jam.

'Are you hungry, little friend?' she asked.

'I would love to share some of that with you,' he replied, and they both set to till they had finished the very last crumb.

'Now,' said the bird, 'this is what you have to do. As you walk along you must pick up anything which you think might prove useful to you in some way. When the right moment comes, your kind heart will tell you just what to do with them. *Remember*, you *will* be back safe and sound, and I shall be there when you return.'

The little girl left her friend reluctantly, and stepped

95

forward as bravely as she could on the path towards the hut on hens' legs. Very soon she caught sight of a handkerchief, neatly folded and held down at one corner by a stone. She picked it up and put it carefully in her pocket. On the branches further along were two ribbons tangled up. She untangled them and placed these, too, in her pocket. The next thing that caught her eye was a tiny tin of oil. 'I can't think why that could be of any use,' said the little girl to herself, but she picked it up just the same and put it, upright, so that it would not spill, into a separate pocket. Next she found a juicy-looking bone. She picked that up too, as well as a large maple-leaf besprinkled with some appetizing-looking bits of meat. She wrapped the leaf around them and carried the bundle in her hand.

And now, straight ahead, she espied the iron gates and through the gates the dreaded hut that moved around on hens' legs. There was a howling wind which made the branches of the birch trees blow helplessly in all directions. The little girl remembered the ribbons she had picked up. 'I'll use them,' she thought, 'to tie round the branches, so they won't lash my face as I pass.' No sooner had she done so than the wind dropped and the branches now swayed gracefully as though dancing to the gentle soughing of the breeze through the leaves. Treading gingerly through the trees, she reached the gates, but when she began to open them they let out a creaking and groaning which made her remember the oil she had picked up. She poured some on all the hinges, after which the gates opened in a peaceful silence. To the fierce-looking dog who looked ready to attack her as she entered she threw the juicy bone and then she fearfully approached the steps of the hut. And there,

O Heavens above! on those very steps stood the gruesome figure of BABA YAGA, THE BONY-LEGGED, with the IRON GNASHING TEETH.

'Hullo, niece, hullo, my pretty one,' she said in an astonishingly soft voice, 'you've come for a needle and thread, no doubt. In you come then. You can do some of my spinning for a while.' She turned to her servant-girl. 'Go and get the bath ready,' she told her. 'We've got to get the girl scrubbed all nice and clean. Get along then, you idle-head, and be quick about it!' She pushed the little girl into the house and swept away, leaving both girls looking as wretched as could be. But the servant-girl cheered up when the little girl gave her the prettily embroidered handkerchief. 'Thank you for your kindness,' she murmured. 'I suppose you know, you're in trouble here with that terrible Baba Yaga, but I'll help you all I can. I'll fetch the water for your bath in a sieve, so it will take an endless time to fill.'

The little girl then noticed the skinny black cat in a corner. Half-starved the poor thing looked. She unwrapped the maple-leaf and put down the meat scraps, which the cat gobbled up greedily, licking his chops. Then he spoke. 'You're in trouble, little one,' he said, 'but I'll see to it that you get a chance to escape from the witch. Take this magic towel and comb and run for your life. But keep your ear close to the ground, for Baba Yaga will be pursuing you in her mortar, beating the air with her pestle. When she gets really close to you, throw down the towel, and a wide river will start flowing between you. But still keep your ear close to the ground, for the evil hag may get across. If she does, you must throw down the comb. It will cause a dense forest of entangled trees to spring up which she will never succeed in getting through. And so your life will be saved.'

The little girl was ready to flee, but she remembered the spinning. 'Baba Yaga will see that I'm not at the spinning-wheel,' she said in despair. 'Leave that to me,' said the cat, and he sat down at the wheel, and my! what a tangle he made of the wool! Baba Yaga passed by the window, but so busy was she with her nasty schemes that she didn't even look up as she said, 'Are you spinning, little niece? Are you working the wheel, my pretty one?'

'I *am* spinning, auntie,' said the cat, trying to imitate the little girl's voice. By and by she passed by the window again and repeated her question, but this time, when the cat replied in his own squeaky voice, she shrieked, 'That's not the voice of my little dinner,' and she rushed in, picked up the cat by the scruff of his neck and hurled him across the room.

'You wretch,' she snarled, 'why did you let the girl escape? You should have scratched her eyes out!'

'In all the years I've served you,' said the cat, 'you've given me nothing but dried-up scraps of left-overs, but this kind little girl gave me delicious morsels of meat.'

Then the witch, in great fury, stormed over to the servant-girl and blamed her for the little girl's escape. 'If you had got the bath ready sooner, she would have been scrubbed clean by now, all ready to be eaten.'

'In all the years I've served you,' replied the servant-girl, 'not one single present have you ever thought of giving me, but the little girl with the kind heart gave me this dainty embroidered handkerchief.'

Baba Yaga dashed around like a mad woman, kicking the dog for letting the little girl pass, cursing the gates for opening without creaking, and beating the birch trees for not lashing the little girl's face to stop her getting away.

The dog replied, 'In all the years I've served you you've never given me a bone to chew on, but the little girl with the kind heart gave me a big juicy one with lots of meat on it.'

And the gates replied, 'In all the years we've stood guarding your hut you've never once put oil on our hinges, and so every time we opened or shut we creaked and groaned, and it hurt. But the little girl with the kind heart oiled our hinges so that we now open and shut smoothly and painlessly.'

And then it was the turn of the birch trees. 'In all the years,' they said, 'that we have been growing tall and sturdy, we've been blown and buffeted by every wind, and not once did you tie our branches. But the little girl with the kind heart tied pretty ribbons gently around them.'

Then Baba Yaga jumped into her mortar and, beating the ground with her pestle, went in hot pursuit of the little girl, sweeping away her tracks with her besom. But the little girl had her ear close to the ground listening intently, and when Baba Yaga was nearly right behind her, she threw down the towel, and all at once a wide rushing river came flowing between them, which the witch could not cross. Back she flew to her yard, gathered all her oxen together and drove them furiously to the river. Nearer and nearer she was getting to the little girl, who was running as fast as her legs could carry her. She could hear the witch behind her, and so she flung down the comb. Then a forest sprang up behind her so thick and tangled that the witch, try as she might with every tool she could find, and even

100

using her iron teeth, was powerless to do anything. Screaming with thwarted rage, she at last gave up and turned back, defeated, to her hen-legged hut.

The little girl only just succeeded in reaching her house and fell, quite breathless, at her father's feet, sobbing piteously and looking as pale as death. Her poor father had no idea what had happened, but when his little daughter had recovered sufficiently she told him the whole story from the very beginning. Her father hugged her tight and promised that never again would she have to fear her wicked stepmother. He drove that evil woman out of the house into the woods, and when they reached the dense forest which had sprung up thanks to the magic comb, he gave her one mighty shove right into the thick of it and – maybe this was due to the magic of the comb – she was able to work her way through the tangle to her sister's hut on hens' legs, but she could *not*, in a thousand years, get back to the side where the little girl and her father lived.

The little girl had not forgotten her friend the nightingale, and when she ran to the woodshed, there he was tapping on the window-pane. From that day onward the nightingale visited them every day; nuts, berries and bits of bacon rind were always waiting for him on the window-sill. As the little girl and her father sat at a table piled high with buttered bread and gooseberry jam, the bird would enjoy his own feast at the window. He would sing his sweetest songs for them and the little girl would tell him her thoughts and all that had happened to her. And the three of them lived happily for the rest of their days.

ALEKSANDR AFANASIEV
(*slightly adapted*)

Little Red Riding Hood
(Little Redcap)

Once upon a time there lived a sweet little girl whom everyone loved as soon as they saw her, but most of all her grandmother, who was for ever trying to find some new present to give her. Once she gave her a little hood of red velvet and as it suited her so well and since she would wear no other, the only name she came to be known by was Little Red Riding Hood.

One day her mother said to her, 'Here is a cake and a bottle of wine. I want you to take it to your grandmother, who is weak and poorly. It will make her feel much better. Now, set out before it gets too warm, and remember what you're about, and don't stray from the path in case you fall and break the bottle, and then Grandmother won't get anything. And when you get to her cottage don't forget to say "Good-day" and don't go staring in every corner.'

'I shall do everything as you say, Mother,' said Little Red Riding Hood, and waved goodbye.

Little Red Riding Hood's grandmother lived some way out in the woods, a good half-hour from the village. And as the little girl came to the woods, whom should she meet but the wolf. But as she didn't know what a wicked creature he was, she wasn't in the least afraid of him.

'Good-day, Little Red Riding Hood,' said he.

'And a good day to you.'

'Where are you off to so early, Little Red Riding Hood?'

'To Grandmother's.'

'What are you carrying under your apron?'

'Cake and wine. We did some baking yesterday, and we hope it will do my poor, weak grandmother good and give her strength.'

'Where does your grandmother live, Little Red Riding Hood?'

'A good quarter of an hour's walk further into the woods. Her cottage stands under three great oak trees, not far from some nut bushes which you'll easily recognize.'

The wolf was thinking to himself, 'She's a nice tender young thing; she'll make a juicy mouthful, much tastier than the old woman. If I act with cunning I'll be able to snap them both up.'

He walked alongside Little Red Riding Hood for a while; then he said, 'Just look at all those lovely flowers growing all around here. You don't seem to notice things; I don't believe you can hear how prettily the birds are twittering. You simply walk on just as though you were on your way to school. Everything here in the woods is so cheerful.'

Little Red Riding Hood opened her eyes, and when she saw the sunbeams dancing hither and thither and all the beautiful flowers, she thought to herself, 'If I take my grandmother a fresh posy of flowers it will certainly gladden her heart. It is still quite early in the day and I can easily reach her cottage in time.' So she ran off the path, right into the woods, and looked about for flowers. But once she had picked one she thought she could see an even prettier one further away and then an even prettier one still further away.

And so she plunged deeper and deeper into the woods.

But the wolf kept straight on in the direction of the grandmother's cottage. And when he got there, he knocked at the door.

'Who's there?'

'Little Red Riding Hood. I'm bringing you cake and wine. Open the door.'

'Just lift the latch,' Grandmother called out. 'I'm too weak to get up.'

The wolf lifted the latch, the door sprang open, and in he went without saying a word, straight to Grandmother's bed, and gobbled her up. Then he dressed himself in her clothes, put her bonnet on his head, lay down in the bed and drew the bed curtains around him.

Little Red Riding Hood, in the meantime, had been running about collecting flowers, and when she had picked so many that she couldn't carry any more, she remembered her grandmother and went back to the path leading to her cottage. She wondered why the door was wide open, and when she stepped into the room such an odd feeling came over her that she thought, 'Heavens above! How worried I'm feeling today, and yet usually I'm so happy to be at Grandmother's.'

She called out, 'Good morning!' but got no reply. So she went up to the bed and drew back the bed curtains. There lay Grandmother, her bonnet pulled low down over her face, looking very strange indeed. 'Oh Grandmother! What big ears you have!'

'All the better to hear you with.'

'Oh Grandmother! What big eyes you have!'

'All the better to see you with.'

104

'Oh Grandmother! What big hands you have!'

'All the better to hold you with.'

'But, Grandmother, what terribly big teeth you have!'

'All the better to eat you with.' And hardly were these last words out of the wolf's mouth when he sprang out of bed and gobbled up poor Little Red Riding Hood.

As soon as he had thus satisfied his appetite, the wolf lay down once more in the bed, fell asleep and started snoring very loudly. A huntsman who happened to be passing by just at that moment thought to himself, 'What a powerful snore the old lady has! I'd better go in and see if there's anything wrong.' So he went into the house, and as he approached the bed he saw the wolf lying in it. 'Ah, so this is where you are, you old rascal. I've been looking for you for months.' But just as he was about to take aim, it occurred to him that the wolf might have swallowed the old grandmother and he might just have time to save her. 'I won't shoot,' he thought, 'I'll get a pair of scissors and slit open the wolf's belly while he's still asleep.' And when he had made a few cuts he saw the gleam of a little red hood, and after a few more cuts the little girl jumped out, crying, 'Oh dear, how scared I was! How dark it was inside the wolf's belly!' And then the old grandmother stepped out, alive and well, though somewhat breathless.

Then Little Red Riding Hood quickly fetched some big stones and filled the wolf's belly with them. The wolf awoke, but when he tried to leap at her, the stones were too heavy for him and he fell back – dead.

So now all three were happy. The huntsman skinned the wolf and took the hide back home with him.

Grandmother ate the cake and drank the wine that Little Red Riding Hood had brought and soon recovered her old strength. But Little Red Riding Hood thought, 'As long as I live, I'll never again run off the path into the woods, and I'll always listen to what Mother tells me.'

THE BROTHERS GRIMM

Thumbelina

Once upon a time there was a woman who dearly wished to have a wee little child, but she didn't know where to get one. So she went to an old witch and said to her, 'I wish so much to have a little child. Will you not tell me where I may get one?'

'Oh yes,' said the witch, 'we can do that. Here's a barleycorn for you – not the sort that grows in farmers' fields or that chickens eat. Put it in a flower-pot and you'll soon have something to look at.'

'Thank you very much,' said the woman, and she gave the witch twelve pence, went home and planted the barleycorn. Very soon a beautiful big flower grew out of it, looking just like a tulip. But the leaves were closed tight, as if it were still in bud.

'That's a lovely flower,' said the woman and kissed it on its pretty red and yellow petals. And just as she kissed it, the flower opened with a loud pop! You could see it was a real tulip, but right in the centre, on a green stool, sat a tiny little girl, so pretty and so delicate, and not much taller than half your thumb. So the woman named her Thumbelina. She gave her a dainty, polished walnut shell for her cradle, blue velvet leaves for mattresses and a rose leaf for her coverlet. There she slept at night, but in the daytime she played on the table, where the woman had put a little plate encircled by a whole wreath of flowers with their stalks in water. A large tulip leaf floated on the water and Thumbelina could sit on it and sail from one side of the plate to the other. And she was given two white horse-hairs to use as oars. It all looked charming. Thumbelina could sing, too, as prettily as you could wish.

One night as she lay on her pretty bed, a nasty toad hopped inside through a broken pane in the window. It was big and fat and wet, and it came hopping on to the table, where Thumbelina lay sleeping under the red rose leaf.

'She would make a nice wife for my son,' thought the toad, and so she took hold of the walnut shell where Thumbelina was sleeping and hopped back through the window down into the garden. Nearby flowed a wide brook with marshy, muddy banks, and this is where the toad lived with her son. Ugh! He was vile and ugly, too, like his mother. All he could say was, 'Croak! Croak! Brek-croak!' when he saw the pretty little girl in the walnut shell.

'Don't talk so loud!' said his mother, 'or you'll wake her. She could easily run away from us, for she's as light as swansdown. We'll put her on one of the big water-lily leaves in the brook, she's so tiny and light it will seem like an island to her. She won't run away then, and in the meantime we shall get the living room ready under the mud, where you can live and build a bigger house.'

Out on the brook there were many water-lilies with broad leaves, that looked as though they were floating on the water. The leaf that was furthest away was also the largest. The mother toad swam out to it and placed Thumbelina on it in her walnut shell. The poor thing woke up very early next morning and when she saw where she was she began to cry bitterly, for all round the big leaf there was water and she couldn't possibly reach the land.

The mother toad sat down on the mud and decorated her room with sedge and reeds, ready for her new daughter-in-law. Then she swam out with her son to the leaf where Thumbelina was. They had come to fetch her little bed, which was to be put in the bridal chamber before she herself came there. The mother toad made a deep curtsey in the water before Thumbelina and said, 'This is my son. He is to be your husband and you will live happily together down in the mud.' 'Croak, croak, brek-croak,' was all her son could say.

So they took the pretty little bed and swam off with it, while Thumbelina sat alone on the green leaf and cried, for she didn't want to live with the nasty mother or to have her ugly son as a husband. The little fishes swimming below in the water had seen the toad and heard what she had said, so they poked their heads up to see the little girl. When they saw her they thought her so beautiful that it hurt them to think she had to go down to the ugly toad in the mud. That must never happen! So they gathered together down in the water round the green stalk that held the leaf Thumbelina was on, and bit away at it with their tiny teeth till the leaf went floating down the brook, carrying the little girl far, far away, where the toads could not reach her. Away sailed Thumbelina past one town after another. The little birds in the bushes saw her and sang, 'What a lovely little girl!'

The leaf floated on, bearing her further and further away, and in this way Thumbelina travelled far out into the country. A pretty little white butterfly kept

hovering around her head and finally sat down on the leaf next to her, for it had taken a liking to Thumbelina, who herself was highly pleased, for now she was out of reach of the toads. It was so pleasant where she was sailing; the sun shone on the water, making it look like liquid gold. She removed the ribbon from round her waist and tied one end of it round the butterfly and the other end to the leaf, so that now it went much faster.

Suddenly a large cockchafer came flying by. He saw Thumbelina and in a flash fastened his claws round her slender waist and flew up with her into a tree. The green leaf went on floating down the brook with the butterfly attached to it, for it could not free itself. Heavens! How scared Thumbelina was when the cockchafer flew up into the tree with her! But she was sorry for the beautiful white butterfly which she had tied to the leaf – if it could not break free, it would starve to death. The cockchafer, however, was not concerned about that at all. He sat down with her on the largest leaf and brought her honey to eat and told her she was very pretty, though not in the least like a cockchafer.

Soon after, all the other cockchafers in the tree called to pay her a visit. They looked at Thumbelina and the lady cockchafers drew in their antennae and said, 'She's only got two legs, it's pitiful! She's got no antennae! Her waist is so skinny! Ugh! She looks more like a human being. How terribly ugly she is!' Yet Thumbelina was, of course, as pretty as a picture. And though the cockchafer who had carried her off still thought her beautiful, when all the others said she was ugly, he, too, now began to think they were right and would have nothing more to do with her – she could go wherever she pleased! They flew down from the

tree with her and sat her on a daisy and there she
stayed and cried, because she was so ugly that even
the cockchafers wouldn't have her. But, of course, she
was the prettiest creature imaginable – graceful, delicate, and as transparent as the most exquisite rose leaf.

All the summer through poor Thumbelina lived
alone in the forest. She plaited herself a bed of green
stalks and hung it up under a large dark leaf so that no
rain might fall on her. She gathered honey from the
flowers and every morning drank the dew which lay
on the leaves. In this way she spent the summer and
autumn, but then winter came – the long, cold winter.
The birds which had sung so sweetly for her flew away
on their long journeys. The trees and flowers withered, the large dark leaf which she had lived under
shrivelled up and became nothing but a yellow, withered stem, and she felt frightfully cold, for her clothes
were now all torn and she herself was so tiny and frail.
Poor Thumbelina! Was she to freeze to death? It
started to snow and every snowflake that fell on her
was like a whole shovelful thrown at one of us – for we
are tall while she was barely an inch high. She
wrapped herself in a withered leaf but that gave her no
warmth. She shivered with cold.

Quite close to the wood where she now was lay a
large cornfield, but the corn had been cut long ago and
only bare dry stubble stood up out of the frozen earth.
To her this seemed like a whole forest to wander
through and, oh! how she shivered with the cold! At
long last she came to the door of a field mouse's home.
It was only a hole in the stubble, but in it the field
mouse lived snug and cosy – she had a room full of
corn, a fine kitchen and a dining room. Poor Thumbelina stood in the doorway like a beggar girl and

begged for a little bit of barleycorn, for she hadn't had anything to eat at all for two days.

'You poor little thing,' said the field mouse, for she was really very kind-hearted, 'do come into my warm room and dine with me.' And as she decided she liked Thumbelina, she added, 'You are most welcome to spend the winter with me, only you must keep my rooms nice and tidy and tell me stories.' Thumbelina did everything the kind field mouse required of her and had a most agreeable time.

'We'll be having a visitor very soon,' said the field mouse one day. 'My neighbour is in the habit of calling on me every week. He is even better off than I am; he has large rooms and goes about in a splendid black velvet coat. If only you would have him as a husband, you would be well looked after. But he cannot see. You must tell him the prettiest stories you know.'

But Thumbelina didn't care for this idea; she didn't want the neighbour for a husband, for he was a mole. He came to pay a visit in his black velvet coat. He was very well-to-do and extremely learned. His manor house, the field mouse had said, was more than twenty times bigger than hers. But in spite of his learning, he had no liking for the sun or for pretty flowers. He spoke ill of them, although he had never seen them. Thumbelina had to sing for both the field mouse and the mole and she sang 'Fly away, fly away, cockchafer' and 'The monk goes walking in the meadow'.

The mole immediately fell in love with her and her pretty voice but he said not a word about it, being a very cautious creature. He had lately burrowed a long passage through the earth from his dwelling to theirs and granted Thumbelina and the field mouse permission to take a walk in it whenever they wished. But he begged

them not to take fright at the dead bird which lay in
the passage; it had been dead only a few days and was
still whole and had all its feathers. It had been buried
in the spot where he had dug his passage. The mole
then took a piece of rotting wood in his mouth (in the
dark this shines just like fire) and lighted the way for
them through the long dark passage till they came to
the spot where the bird lay. Then the mole pushed his
broad nose through the earth ceiling, making a hole
which let in the light. There, on the earth floor, lay a
dead swallow, its pretty wings pressed fast to its sides
and its legs tucked under its feathers. The poor bird
must have died of cold. The sight made Thumbelina
very sad, for she loved all the birds which had sung so
prettily to her through the summer. The mole pushed
at it with his short leg and said, 'It won't chirp any
more. It must be wretched to be born a little bird.
Heaven be praised that none of my children will come
to this. A bird such as this has nothing except its tweet
tweet, and so is sure to die of hunger in the winter.'

'Yes indeed,' said the field mouse. 'You speak like a
reasonable man. What *has* a bird got, for all its tweet
tweet, when winter comes? It must starve and freeze.
Why it is considered such a pretty thing, I really don't
know.'

Thumbelina didn't say anything, but when their
backs were turned, she bent down, parted the feathers
on the bird's head and kissed the closed eyes. 'Maybe
this was the one that sang so sweetly to me through
the summer,' she thought. 'What happiness you gave
me, dear beautiful bird!'

The mole now stopped up the hole which let the
daylight through and escorted the ladies home. But
that night Thumbelina couldn't sleep a wink. She got

out of bed and plaited a beautiful coverlet of hay, carried it down and spread it round the dead bird. Then she placed some soft cotton, which she had found in the field mouse's room, against the bird's sides so that it could lie warm on the cold earth.

'Goodbye, beautiful bird,' she said, 'goodbye and thank you for your sweet song in the summer when all the trees were green and the sun shone so warm upon us.' She laid her head upon the bird's breast, but in doing so she got quite a shock, for there was something ticking away inside! It was the bird's heart! The swallow was not dead: it had only been numbed by the cold and now that it was warmed up it had revived!

In the autumn all swallows fly off to warm lands, but if one of them lags behind, the cold becomes too much for it, so that it falls down quite dead and is covered by the snow.

Thumbelina was shivering all over; she was so frightened for, compared with her, who was barely an inch high, the bird was really huge. But she plucked up courage, arranged the cotton closer round the poor swallow, fetched a curled mint leaf, which she herself used as a coverlet, and placed it over the bird's head. Next night she stole down to it again, and there it was, quite alive, but so weak that it opened its eyes only for a second and looked at Thumbelina standing there with a piece of withered wood in her hand – for she had no other light.

'Thank you, sweet child,' said the sick bird. 'I am quite warm now. I shall soon get back my strength and fly off again into the warm sunshine.'

'Oh!' said Thumbelina, 'but it is so very cold outside. It's snowing and freezing. Please stay here in your warm bed and let me look after you.' She brought the swallow some water on a leaf. It drank it and told her that it had scratched its wing on a thorn bush and therefore could not fly as strongly as the other birds when they had set off to fly far away to warmer lands. At long last it had fallen to the ground and couldn't remember any more. It didn't know how it had got where it now was.

But there it stayed all the winter, and Thumbelina was very kind to it and became very attached to it. Both the mole and the field mouse ignored it completely; they hated the poor, wretched swallow.

When spring came and the sun had warmed the earth, the swallow said goodbye to Thumbelina. She opened up the hole which the mole had made above and the glorious sunlight poured through. The swallow asked her if she wouldn't like to go away with it: she could sit on its back and they would fly far out into the green woods. But Thumbelina said it would upset the old field mouse if she were to leave like that. 'No,' she said, 'I cannot come.'

'Goodbye, kind, sweet girl!' said the swallow and flew away into the sunshine. Thumbelina watched it as it flew further and further away into the distance, and tears came to her eyes, for she dearly loved the poor swallow. 'Tweet tweet,' sang the bird and flew off into the green woods.

Thumbelina was very sad. She wasn't allowed to go out into the warm sunshine. The corn which had been sown in the field above the field mouse's house had shot up so high it was like a dense forest to our tiny girl who was barely an inch tall.

'You must set about making your trousseau this summer,' the field mouse told her, for their neighbour, the dreary old mole in the black velvet coat, had asked for her hand in marriage.

'You must have both linens and woollens, where you can sit and lie when you are married,' the field mouse added.

So Thumbelina was obliged to spin on the distaff, and the field mouse engaged four spiders to weave for her day and night.

The mole came to pay a visit every evening and always talked about how, when the summer was over, the sun wouldn't shine half as warmly as now, when it was baking the earth hard as stone. Yes, indeed, when summer was over the marriage with Thumbelina would take place. But she wasn't at all happy, for there was nothing whatsoever about the dreary old mole that she could possibly like. Every morning when the sun rose and each evening when it set, she would steal out through the doorway, and when the wind blew through the tops of the corn, allowing her to glimpse the blue sky, she thought how beautiful it must be outside. And she longed to see her dear swallow again. But it never came back; it must have flown far, far away into the green woods.

When autumn came Thumbelina's trousseau was all ready.

'In four weeks' time the wedding will take place,' said the field mouse, but Thumbelina wept and said she didn't want to marry the dreary old mole.

'Stuff and nonsense!' said the field mouse. 'Don't be so wayward or I shall bite you with my white teeth! You'll be getting a first-rate husband. Not even the queen has a black velvet coat like his. And he has lots of things in his cellar, and in his kitchen, too! You ought to thank God for such a husband!'

So the marriage was to take place. The mole was not slow in coming to fetch Thumbelina; she was to live with him deep down under the earth, never to come up to the warm sunshine, for he didn't care for the sun. The poor child was upset beyond words; she was now to say goodbye for ever to the beautiful sun – which she had at least been allowed to glimpse through the field mouse's doorway.

'Goodbye, goodbye, bright sun,' she said and stretched her arms high up in the air. Then she walked a little outside the field mouse's house, for the corn had now been reaped and there was nothing left but dry stubble.

'Goodbye, goodbye,' she said and put her arms round a little red flower that grew there. 'Give my greeting to the dear swallow if you chance to see it.'

Suddenly she heard a tweet tweet above her head. She looked up and there was the swallow flying by! When it saw Thumbelina it was overjoyed. She told the swallow how loth she was to have the ugly mole for a husband and how she would have to live deep under the earth where the sun never shone. She couldn't help crying at the mere thought of it.

'The cold winter will soon be upon us,' said the swallow. 'I am flying far away to warmer lands. Will you come with me? You can sit on my back. Only you must tie yourself tight with your waist-ribbon and then we'll fly far, far away – far from the ugly mole and his dark room, far beyond the mountains to the lands where the sun shines more brightly than here, to lands where there are beautiful flowers and where it is always summer. Please fly away with me, dear, sweet little Thumbelina – you who saved my life when I was frozen in the cellar beneath the earth!'

'Yes, I will come with you,' said Thumbelina. She sat herself on the bird's back, placed her little feet on its outspread wings, tied her ribbon fast to one of its strongest feathers, and the swallow flew off high in the air, over forests and lakes, over high, ever snow-capped mountains. Thumbelina shivered in the freezing air, so she crept under the bird's warm feathers, only keeping out her little head to gaze at the beauty below.

At long last they reached the warm lands. There the sun shone bright and the sky seemed twice as lofty, and in the ditches and on the fences grew the most beautiful green and purple grapes. In the woods hung oranges and lemons, there was a scent of curly mint, and among the woods ran the prettiest children chasing brightly coloured butterflies. As the swallow flew further the scene grew more and more beautiful. Under some majestic green trees near a blue lake stood a palace, gleaming white, built in ancient times, surrounded by lofty pillars entwined with vine leaves. In the tops of these pillars were many swallows' nests and one of them was the home of the swallow which was carrying Thumbelina.

'Here is my house,' said the swallow. 'Choose for yourself one of the splendid flowers growing beneath it and I will set you down on it and you will be as happy as you could wish to be.'

'That will be wonderful!' said Thumbelina, clapping her hands.

Down on the ground lay a huge white marble pillar. It had fallen and broken into three fragments, among which grew the most dazzlingly white flowers. The swallow flew down with Thumbelina and placed her on one of the broad leaves. Imagine her astonishment when she saw, in the centre of the flower, a little man, as white and transparent as if he were made of glass! On his head was the most charming gold crown and on his shoulders the prettiest bright wings. He was no bigger than Thumbelina. He was the 'angel of the flower' – there was one in each blossom, a little man or a little woman – but this one was the king of them all.

'Goodness me! How handsome he is!' whispered Thumbelina to the swallow. But the little king was frightened by the swallow, for next to him it seemed like some giant bird, while he was so tiny and graceful. But when he saw Thumbelina he was very happy, for she was by far the most beautiful creature he had ever seen. He took his gold crown off his head and placed it on hers, asked her what her name was and if she would be his wife, for then she would be queen of all the flowers. Here indeed was a real husband! Quite different from the toad's son or the mole with the black velvet coat. So she said yes to the handsome prince, and then out of every flower came a lady or lord, a delight to look upon. Each one brought Thumbelina a gift, but best of all was a pair of beautiful wings from a splendid white fly. They were fastened on to Thumbelina's back, so now she, too, could fly from flower to flower. There was much rejoicing; the little swallow sat in its nest and sang its loveliest song, though at heart it was sad, for it loved Thumbelina and wished never to be far away from her.

'You shall not be called Thumbelina,' said the 'angel of the flower' to her. 'It's not a pretty name and you are *very* pretty! We shall call you Maia.'

'Goodbye, goodbye,' said the swallow and flew away once more, away from the warm lands back to Denmark. There it had a little nest above the window of the house where the man who can tell stories lives. And to him it sang tweet tweet, and that is how he learned the whole story.

HANS CHRISTIAN ANDERSEN

The Three Wishes

Once upon a time there lived a poor man and his pretty wife, and as they sat by their fire one winter evening they began talking about the happiness of their neighbours, who were richer than they were.

'Oh! if only I could have everything I wished,' said the wife, 'I'd be happier than all those folk.'

'So should I,' said the husband.

At that instant a most beautiful lady appeared before them and spoke to them thus:

'I am a fairy. I promise to grant you the first three things you ask for. But take care; once you have wished for three things, there is nothing more I can grant you.'

The fairy vanished, and the man and his wife couldn't make up their minds what to wish for.

'As far as I am concerned,' said the wife, 'I know very well what I should like. I'm not making my wish just yet, but it seems to me that there is nothing as good as being beautiful and rich and being a lady of high rank.'

'But,' replied the husband, 'if one *were* all those things, there's still the chance of becoming ill and unhappy. And one could die young. It would be wiser to wish for health, joy and a long life.'

'And what would be the use of a long life if one were poor?' retorted the wife. 'Really the fairy should have granted us a dozen gifts.'

'True enough,' agreed the husband, 'but let's take our time. From now till tomorrow morning let's think carefully about the three things we are most in need of and then we shall ask for them. Meanwhile, let's warm ourselves, it's getting very cold.'

The wife picked up the tongs and stirred up the fire, and when she saw the coals burning brightly, she said without thinking, 'Now there's a nice fire, I wish we had a yard of black pudding for our supper, we could cook it quite easily.'

Hardly had she spoken these words when a yard of black pudding came tumbling down the chimney.

'A plague on you with your black pudding!' cried her husband. 'That's a fine wish you've gone and made! Now we've only two wishes left. I wish the black pudding were on the tip of your nose!'

At once the man realized that he had been even sillier than his wife, for the pudding instantly jumped to the tip of the poor woman's nose, and she couldn't pull it away.

'Oh, wretched creature that I am!' she exclaimed. 'You are a bad man to have wished the pudding on to my nose!'

'I swear to you, my dear wife, that I did not intend it,' said her husband. 'I am going to wish that we had great riches and I shall make you a gold case to hide that pudding.'

'Just you beware of doing that,' said his wife, 'for I should kill myself if I had to live with a thing like that on my nose. We have one wish left. Let me make it, or I shall throw myself out of the window.'

With these words she ran to open the window, but the husband, who loved his wife, cried out, 'Wait, my dear wife, I give you leave to wish whatever you like.'

'Very well,' said the wife, 'I wish this pudding to fall to the ground.'

And at that very instant the pudding came away from her nose, and the woman, who was no fool, said, 'That fairy has made us look silly, and she was quite right. If we were richer than we are now, we should perhaps be more unhappy. Believe me, my dear, let's not wish for anything, but take what it will please God to send us. And meanwhile let us have our pudding for supper, since that's all we have left of our wishes.'

The husband thought his wife was right. They ate their supper with a light heart and never again tormented themselves by wishing for impossible things.

MADAME LE PRINCE DE BEAUMONT

Snow-White and
the Seven Dwarfs

Once upon a time in the depth of winter a queen sat
sewing by her window, which was framed in black
ebony, and watched the snowflakes as they fluttered
like feathers from the sky to the earth below. And as
she sewed and gazed at the snow, she pricked her
finger with a needle and three drops of blood fell upon
the snow. The red on the white snow looked very
beautiful and it made her think: 'If only I had a child
white as snow and red as blood and dark as the ebony
frame of this window.' Soon afterwards she gave birth
to a little daughter who was indeed white as snow, red
as blood and dark-haired as ebony wood, and because
of this she was called Little Snow-White. But the
queen died as the child was born.

After a year or so the king took himself another wife.
She was a beautiful woman, but she was proud and
arrogant and she could not bear to be surpassed in
beauty by anyone else. She had a wonderful magic
mirror, and when she stood in front of it and looked at
herself and said:

> *Mirror, mirror, on the wall,*
> *Who is the fairest of them all?*

the mirror would reply:

My Lady Queen, you are the fairest one of all.

Then she was happy, for she knew that the mirror told the truth.

Little Snow-White was now growing up and becoming lovelier every day, and when she was seven years of age she was as beautiful as a bright clear day and more beautiful than the queen herself. And when the queen next asked the mirror:

> *Mirror, mirror, on the wall,*
> *Who is the fairest of them all?*

the mirror replied:

> *My Lady Queen, of beauty rare,*
> *Snow-White's a thousand times more fair.*

Then the queen was filled with horror and turned green and yellow with envy, and from that moment every time she saw Little Snow-White her heart turned over inside her, she so hated the girl. Her envy and arrogance grew like a weed in her heart, so that she could not rest by day or night.

One day she summoned a huntsman and told him, 'Take the child outside into the forest, I cannot bear the sight of her any longer. See that she is killed, and bring her lungs and liver to me as a sign that you have carried out my order.' The huntsman obeyed and took the child away, but when he had drawn his hunting-knife and was about to pierce the innocent child's heart, she began to weep and said, 'Ah, dear huntsman, let me live; I will run into the wild forest and never come back home again.' And she looked so beautiful that the huntsman took pity on her. 'Run off

126

then, you poor child,' he said. He thought to himself, 'The wild beasts will have eaten you up soon enough,' and yet he felt as though a heavy stone had rolled away from his heart because he had not needed to kill her. And as a young wild boar happened to spring into view just at that moment, he stabbed it, took out its lungs and liver, and fetched them to the queen as a sign that he had obeyed her order. The cook was ordered to stew them in salt and the wicked queen ate them, thinking she had eaten Little Snow-White's lungs and liver.

Now the poor child was all alone in the great forest, and she was so terrified that she seemed to look at every leaf on the trees in a vain effort to find a way out. Then she began to run and run, over sharp stones and through spiky thorns, and wild beasts sprang past her but did her no harm. On and on she fled, till her legs could carry her no longer, and just as it was getting dark she espied a tiny house, and she went inside to rest. In the house everything was very small, but so neat and dainty it was hard to believe. There was a little table covered with a white cloth and laid with seven little plates, each plate with its little spoon, its little knife and fork, and seven little goblets. Along the wall stood seven little beds next to one another, each covered with a snow-white sheet.

As she was so hungry and thirsty, Little Snow-White ate a little of the bread and salad from each plate and drank a little drop of wine from each little goblet, because she didn't want to take everything just from one. And then, because she felt so tired, she lay down in a little bed, but not one of the beds suited her; one was too long, another too short; till at last the seventh was just right, and there she lay, put herself in God's hands and fell asleep.

When it had become quite dark the masters of this little house came home; they were seven dwarfs whose work was digging and burrowing for ore in the mountains. They lit their seven little lamps, and as it was now light in the little house they saw that someone had been in, for everything was not as tidy as they had left it. The first one said, 'Who has been sitting in my little chair?' The second, 'Who has eaten from my little plate?' The third, 'Who has taken some of my little loaf?' The fourth, 'Who has been eating my little salad?' The fifth, 'Who has been pricking with my little fork?' The sixth, 'Who has been cutting with my little knife?' And the seventh, 'Who has been drinking from my little goblet?' Then the first one looked around and saw there was a little hollow in his bed and he said, 'Who has been getting into my little bed?' The others came running up, crying, 'Someone has been lying in my bed too.' But the seventh, when he looked at his bed, saw Little Snow-White lying in it asleep. And so he called the others, who came running up, crying out in amazement. They fetched their little lamps and gazed in wonder at Little Snow-White. 'Oh, my good Lord! My good Lord!' they cried. 'What a beautiful child!' And they were so full of joy that they did not wake her but let her sleep on in the little bed. But the seventh slept with his fellow dwarfs, one hour with each, till the night was over.

When it was morning Little Snow-White awoke and when she saw the seven dwarfs she was frightened. But they were friendly and asked her, 'What is your name?'

'My name is Little Snow-White,' she replied.

'How did you come upon our house?' they asked

further. Then she told them that her stepmother had wanted to kill her but that the huntsman had spared her life, and then she had run the whole day long until at last she had found their little house. Then the dwarfs asked her, 'Will you be our housekeeper, cook and make the beds, wash and sew and knit for us, and will you keep everything neat and tidy? If you will, you can stay and live with us and you shall have everything you need.'

'Yes,' said Little Snow-White, 'with all my heart.' And so she stayed with them.

She kept everything neat and tidy for them. In the morning they would go out into the mountains, looking for ore and gold, and in the evening they would come back and their meals had to be ready for them. But during the day the girl was all alone and the kind dwarfs warned her, 'Be on your guard against your stepmother; she will soon find out that you are here. Don't let anyone in.'

The queen, however, after she had eaten what she believed to be Little Snow-White's lungs and liver, had no doubt whatsoever that she was once more the most beautiful of all. She stood in front of her mirror and said:

> *Mirror, mirror, on the wall,*
> *Who is the fairest of them all?*

And the mirror answered:

> *My Lady Queen is fair indeed*
> *But this, in truth, all will concede,*
> *That o'er the hills, in dwarfs' kind care,*
> *Snow-White's the fairest of the fair.*

At this the queen was horrified, for she knew that the mirror told no untruth and she realized that the huntsman had deceived her and that Little Snow-White was still alive. And so she brooded and thought and thought of some new way of destroying her once and for all, for as long as she herself was not the most beautiful in the whole land, her jealousy would give her no peace. And when at last she had thought of a plan, she painted her face and disguised herself as an old pedlar-woman so that no one could recognize her. Dressed up like this she went across the seven mountains to the home of the seven dwarfs, knocked at the door and called, 'Fine wares, fine wares, fine wares for sale!' Little Snow-White looked out of the window and cried, 'Good day, kind lady, what things have you to sell?'

'Fine goods, excellent wares,' she replied, 'ribbon-lacing of every colour,' and she brought one out which was woven of gaily-coloured silk.

'There could be no harm in letting this honest woman in,' thought Little Snow-White, and she unlatched the door and bought the pretty ribbon-lace.

'Child!' said the old woman. 'What a sight you look! Come, let me lace you up properly.'

Little Snow-White, not suspecting a thing, stood in front of her and let the old woman lace up her bodice with the new ribbon. But the old woman laced fast and laced so tight that Little Snow-White lost her breath and fell down as if dead.

'Now,' said the old woman, 'you *were* the fairest in the land, but no longer,' and she rushed out.

Not long after, towards evening, the seven dwarfs came back home, and you may imagine how horrified they were when they saw their dear Little Snow-White lying on the floor. She neither moved nor stirred – she was as one dead. They raised her up, and as they saw that she was too tightly laced up they cut the ribbons asunder. She took a short while to get her breath back, and bit by bit she came to life again. When the dwarfs heard what had happened they said, 'That old pedlar-woman was none other than the evil queen; you must take good care and let no one in when we are not near you.'

The wicked woman, however, when she arrived home, went straight to her mirror and asked:

> Mirror, mirror, on the wall,
> Who is the fairest of them all?

And the mirror answered as before:

> My Lady Queen is fair indeed
> But o'er the hills, in dwarfs' kind care,
> Snow-White's the fairest of the fair.

When she heard this, all the blood fled from her heart, so terrorstruck was she, for she well realized that Little Snow-White had once more come back to life. 'Well then,' she said, 'I will think of something that will get rid of you for good and all,' and with the power of witchcraft, the art of which she understood, she made a poisoned comb. Then she disguised herself as a different old woman and went across the seven mountains to the home of the seven dwarfs. She knocked on the door and called out, 'Fine wares, fine wares, fine wares for sale.' Little Snow-White peeped out and said, 'Go away, I must not let anyone in.' 'But surely you are allowed to look,' said the old crone, and took out the poisoned comb and held it up for her to see. The child was so taken by it that she allowed herself to be duped and so she opened the door. As soon as they were agreed on the price, the old woman said, 'Now I am going to comb your hair properly.' Poor Little Snow-White, quite unsuspecting, let the old woman have her way, but hardly had she stuck the comb into her hair when the poison in it began to work and the girl fell down senseless.

'Now, you perfect model of beauty,' said the evil woman, 'that should have got rid of you,' and away she went.

Luckily, however, it was soon evening and the seven dwarfs came back home. When they saw Little Snow-White lying on the floor as though dead, they immediately suspected that the stepmother had been at work again. They found the poisoned comb in her hair, and they had scarcely pulled it out when Little Snow-White came to and told them what had happened. Then they warned her once more to be on her guard and never to open the door to anyone.

Back at her palace the queen once more stood in front of her mirror and said:

> Mirror, mirror, on the wall,
> Who is the fairest of them all?

And the mirror answered as before:

> My Lady Queen is fair indeed
> But this, in truth, all must concede,
> That o'er the hills, in dwarfs' kind care,
> Snow-White's the fairest of the fair.

When she heard the mirror say these words, she trembled and quivered with rage. 'Little Snow-White shall die,' she cried, 'even if it costs me my own life.' Thereupon she went into a quite hidden, secret chamber where nobody ever came, and there she fashioned an apple that was deadly poisoned. On the outside it looked most tempting, white and rosy-cheeked; anyone looking at it would long to eat it, but if they were to take one single bite they were bound to die. When the apple was ready, the queen painted her face and dressed up as a peasant woman, and made her way across the seven mountains to the home of the seven dwarfs. She knocked at the door and Little Snow-White leaned her head out of the window and said, 'I am not permitted to let anyone in, the seven dwarfs have forbidden me.'

'It's no matter to me,' answered the peasant woman, 'I'll soon get rid of my apples, but, never mind, I'll give you one.'

'No,' said Little Snow-White, 'I must not accept anything at all.'

'What,' said the old woman, 'are you afraid you may get poisoned? Just look, I'll cut this apple in two – you shall have the rosy half and I'll eat the white.' For the apple was made so cunningly that only the red half was poisoned. Little Snow-White was simply longing for that lovely apple, and when she saw that the old peasant woman was eating it she couldn't resist any longer and she stretched out her hand and took the poisoned half. No sooner had she taken one bite than she fell lifeless to the ground. The queen gazed at her with a terrifying look and laughed wildly and shrieked, 'White as snow, red as blood, black as ebony! This time the dwarfs will not awaken you!' She hastened home and asked the mirror:

Mirror, mirror, on the wall,
Who is the fairest of them all?

And the mirror at last gave the answer:

My Lady Queen, you are the fairest of them all.

Then was her jealous heart at rest, as far as a jealous heart can ever be at rest.

When the little dwarfs came back to the house in the evening, they found Little Snow-White lying on the ground, no breath coming from her mouth; she was lifeless. They raised her up, searched around to see if they could find anything poisonous, unlaced her, combed her hair, washed her with water and wine, but all to no avail. The dear child was dead and dead she remained.

They laid her on a bier, and all seven of them sat by it and wept for her, and they wept for three whole days. Then they wanted to bury her, but she looked so fresh, like a living person, and she still had her beautiful rosy cheeks. 'We cannot,' they said, 'lay her in the cold black earth.' And they had a transparent coffin of glass made so that she could be seen from every side; and they laid her in it and wrote her name in golden letters on it, saying that she was the daughter of a king. Then they laid the coffin down outside on the mountain and one of them stayed by it always, watching over it. And the animals came too and wept for Little Snow-White, first an owl, then a raven and, last of all, a little dove.

Little Snow-White lay for a long time in the coffin; she never changed but looked as though she were asleep, for she was still as white as snow, as red as blood, and as dark-haired as ebony.

135

Now it so happened that a king's son was out riding in the forest and he came upon the dwarfs' house, where he thought of seeking shelter for the night. He saw the coffin on the mountain and beautiful Snow-White inside, and he read what was written on it in letters of gold.

Then he said to the dwarfs, 'Let me have the coffin. I will give you whatever you ask for it.' But the dwarfs replied, 'We would not part with it for all the gold in the world.' Then he said, 'Well, let me have it as a gift from you, for I cannot live without the sight of Little Snow-White before my eyes. I will honour her and treat her with the deepest regard, as though she were my dearest beloved.' The way he spoke persuaded the kind little dwarfs to take pity on him and they gave him the coffin. The young prince bade his servants carry it away on their shoulders. It so happened that on their way they stumbled over a clump of grass, and the sudden jolt jerked the piece of poisoned apple that Little Snow-White had bitten off out of her throat. And the next moment she opened her eyes, lifted the lid of the coffin, and sat upright, alive once more.

'Merciful heavens, where am I?' she cried. Filled with joy, the young prince said, 'You are with me.' And he told her everything that had taken place and added, 'I love you more than anything else in the world. Come with me to my father's castle and be my wife.' And Little Snow-White fell in love with him, and went with him to his palace. Their wedding was celebrated with great splendour and magnificence.

Little Snow-White's evil stepmother was among the guests invited to the banquet. When she was arrayed in her most beautiful clothes, she stepped in front of the mirror and said:

Mirror, mirror, on the wall,
Who is the fairest of them all?

And the mirror replied:

My Lady Queen is of beauty rare,
But the new young Queen's a thousand times more fair.

Then the wicked woman was beside herself. At first she resolved not to go to the wedding, but that gave her no peace – she simply had to go, in order to see the new young queen. And when she entered the banquet-hall and recognized Little Snow-White, she stood rooted to the spot, unable to move for horror and fear. But iron slippers had already been heated and these were now brought to her. Then she had to step into them, and dance till she fell down dead.

THE BROTHERS GRIMM

Thorn Rose,
the Sleeping Beauty

Once upon a time there lived a king and queen who longed for children but had none. One day when the queen was bathing, a frog hopped out of the water and said: 'Your wish will soon be granted and you will have a daughter.'

So it happened, and the king was so delighted at the birth of the princess that he gave a great feast and invited the fairies who lived in his kingdom. There were thirteen of them altogether, but he was forced to leave one out because he had only twelve gold plates. The fairies came to the feast and at the end they gave gifts to the child. The first gave her goodness, the second beauty, and so on; between them they gave her all that heart could desire.

But just as the eleventh fairy had given her gift the thirteenth arrived. She was furiously angry because she had not been invited and she shrieked: 'Since you didn't ask me to your feast, I tell you this: when your daughter is fifteen she will prick herself with a spindle and she will fall dead.' The king and queen were filled with horror, but the twelfth fairy had not yet made her wish. She said: 'The princess will not die, she will only fall into a deep sleep for a hundred years.'

The king still hoped to save his daughter, and he ordered that every spindle in the kingdom should be destroyed.

The princess grew up and became marvellously beautiful. One day when she was just fifteen she found herself alone in the palace. She wandered about as she pleased and at last she came to an old tower. A winding staircase led up to it, and the princess felt curious. She climbed the stairs and came to a little door with a golden key in the lock.

She turned the key, the door flew open, and she saw a tiny room and an old woman spinning flax. The old woman welcomed her and showed her how to spin. But she had hardly touched the spindle when she pricked herself and at once fell down in a deep sleep.

At that moment the king returned to the palace with his courtiers, and they all fell asleep at once. The horses in the stable, the doves on the roof, the dogs in the kennel, the flies on the wall, even the fire burning in the hearth fell asleep. The meat stopped turning on the spit, and the cook let the kitchenboy go as she was about to box his ears, and the kitchenmaid dropped the hen that she was plucking, and slept.

A hedge of thorns sprang up round the palace and grew higher and higher, so that it was lost to sight.

Princes who had heard of the beautiful Thorn Rose came and tried to rescue her, but none of them could force a way through the hedge.

Many many years passed, and at last another prince who was travelling through that part of the country asked about the thorn hedge. An old man told him the story he had heard from his grandfather. Inside that great hedge, he said, there was a palace where a beautiful princess lay asleep with all her court, and long ago many princes had tried to force their way through, but they were all caught on the thorns and perished miserably.

'But I shall succeed,' said the prince, 'and I shall rescue the lovely Thorn Rose.'

As he came up to the hedge, the thorns turned into flowers that parted to let him through, but behind him thorns closed in again. Then he came to a door.

It opened at his touch and he found himself in the palace courtyard. The horses and hounds were lying asleep and the doves were sitting on the roof with their heads under their wings. As the prince entered the palace he saw the flies asleep on the wall, and in the kitchen the cook and the kitchenmaid and the fire in the hearth were all asleep.

He went on through the palace and saw all the courtiers sleeping, and the king and queen asleep on their throne, and it was so quiet that he could hear his own breathing.

At last he came to the old tower where Thorn Rose lay and slept. The prince was so overcome by her beauty that he bent and kissed her, and in a moment she awoke. So did everyone else, the king and the queen and all the courtiers, the horses and the dogs, the doves on the roof and the flies on the wall.

The fire flamed up and cooked the food, and the meat sizzled on the spit, and the cook boxed the kitchenboy's ears, and the kitchenmaid busily plucked the hen. At the same moment the hedge of thorns vanished away. Then the wedding of the prince and Thorn Rose was celebrated and they lived happily together all their lives.

THE BROTHERS GRIMM

The Frog Prince

In olden times, when wishes often came true, there lived a king whose daughters were all beautiful, but the youngest was so extremely lovely that the sun itself, which had seen much in its time, was lost in admiration every time it shone on her face. Not far from the king's castle lay a great dark forest, and in this forest, under an old linden tree, was a well. Whenever the days were very warm, the king's youngest child would venture out into the forest and sit by the edge of the well to enjoy its cooling freshness. And sometimes, when she'd had enough of sitting still, she would take her golden ball and throw it high up into the air and catch it as it fell. This indeed was her favourite pastime.

It happened one day that the golden ball which the little princess had thrown up high did not fall back into the hand held up to catch it, but on to the ground, where it rolled straight into the well. The princess tried to follow it with her eyes, but it disappeared. The water in the well was quite deep, so deep that you couldn't see the bottom. Then she began to weep. Her weeping grew louder and louder and nothing would comfort her. And as she went on wailing and crying she heard a voice call out to her, 'What ails you, little princess? Your crying would arouse pity in a heart of stone.' She looked round to see where the voice was coming from and espied a frog, its thick, ugly head just above the water.

'Oh it's you, is it, you old water-splasher? I'm crying because my golden ball has fallen into the well.'

'Calm yourself and don't cry,' said the frog. 'I know what to do about that. But first tell me: what will you give me if I fetch your plaything back to you?'

'Whatever you wish, dear frog,' said she. 'My clothes, my pearls and precious stones, and, yes, even the golden crown I'm wearing.'

The frog replied, 'I do not desire your clothes, nor your pearls and precious stones, nor even your golden crown. But if you will love me, and let me be your companion and playmate, and sit at your table next to you and eat from your little golden plate and drink out of your little golden cup and sleep in your warm little bed – if you promise me all that, I will go down to the bottom of the well and fetch you back your golden ball.'

'Oh yes,' she replied, 'I promise you all that, everything you wish, if you will only bring me back my golden ball.' But secretly she thought, 'It's only a stupid frog prattling. He spends his time in the water croaking with his fellow frogs. How can he be a companion to a human being?'

As soon as he had received this promise, the frog headed down into the water, and shortly after came back up, the ball in his mouth, and threw it on to the grass. The king's daughter was overjoyed to see her beautiful plaything back again. She picked it up and ran off with it.

'Wait, wait,' called the frog, 'take me with you. I can't run as fast as you.' But croak, croak as loud as he could after her, it was of no avail. She heard none of it, but hurried back to the palace, putting the poor frog completely out of her mind, and he, of course, had to go back into the waters of the well.

The following day, when the princess, together with her father and all the courtiers, was seated at table and eating from her little golden plate, there was a plitch-plotch, plitch-plotch noise coming up the marble steps of the castle. It stopped at the door and there was a knock, knock, followed by a voice calling, 'Youngest daughter of the king, open the door to me.' She ran out to see who was there and it was none other than the frog. She slammed the door and came back to sit down at the table, looking very ill at ease. The king could sense that her heart was beating violently and said, 'My child, what frightened you so? Is there some giant at the door waiting to carry you off?'

'Oh no,' said she, 'it's no giant, just a horrid nasty frog.'

'What does the frog want from you?'

'Ah, dear father, yesterday when I was in the woods by the well, playing with my golden ball, it fell into the water. And because he saw me weeping, the frog brought it back up for me, and because he kept on asking me I promised him that he could be my companion. I never thought that he would leave the waters of the well. And now he is outside and wants to come in to be with me.'

At that moment there was another knock and a voice called out:

> Little king's daughter, now open your door.
> Remember the promise you yesterday swore
> To let your frog in to sup by your side
> And to sleep in your bed and with you to abide.

Then the king said, 'What you have promised you must stand by. Go now and let him in.'

So she went and opened the door, and the frog hopped inside and followed closely at her heels till they reached her chair. He sat on the floor, but called out, 'Pick me up and place me next to you.' She hesitated, but the king commanded her to do the frog's bidding. But when the frog was seated on a chair he asked to be placed on the table, and when he was there he said, 'Now push your little golden plate near me so that we can eat together.' And this she did indeed, but everyone could see that she did it with great distaste. The frog enjoyed his meal, but the princess struggled with every mouthful.

At last the frog said, 'I have eaten my fill and I'm feeling tired. Take me up to your little bedroom and smooth out the satin covers of your little bed so that I can sleep by your side.'

The princess began to weep, shuddering at the thought of the cold frog, for she could hardly bear even to touch him, and to think of him beside her in her beautiful clean bed! But her tears only made the king more angry, and he said, 'You were helped when you were in trouble, so do not hurt the frog now.'

Then she took hold of the frog gingerly between two fingers, and carried him upstairs to her room, where she placed him in a corner. But when she was lying in bed he crept up to it and said, 'I am tired and I want to sleep as much as you do. Take me up, or I shall tell your father.'

The princess stretched over, picked him up and laid him at the foot of her bed. Then she burst into sobs, buried her face in the pillow and finally fell into a deep sleep. But the next morning, when she awoke, there he was on her little pillow.

And then – with one startling leap on to the floor – there, before the gaze of the astonished princess, stood a handsome young prince. No sign of any frog!

He told her how he had been put under a spell by a malicious witch and changed into a frog, doomed to live in the well till some princess would let him eat out of her plate and sleep in her bed. No one but she could have had the power to break the spell.

'If you will be my bride,' said the prince, 'we will go together to my own kingdom.' The princess had fallen in love with the handsome young man the very moment she had set eyes on him, and her father gladly consented to the marriage.

The next morning, with the rising sun, there drove up to the doors of the king's castle a carriage drawn by eight white horses, their heads adorned with ostrich feathers and gleaming with golden bridles. And behind the carriage stood Henry, the prince's loyal servant. This trusty youth had been so stricken with grief when his master had been changed into a frog that he had bound three iron bands round his heart for fear it should break from sorrow. But now the carriage was all ready to take the prince and his princess back to his kingdom. The faithful Henry helped them in and sat behind, overcome with joy at his master's release from the spell.

When they had driven a little way, the prince heard a crack, as if something were splitting behind him. Turning round, he said to Henry:

The wheels are creaking, Hal, I hear.

To which Henry replied:

THE FROG PRINCE

Nay, nay, my lord need have no fear.
When you to frog were changed by spell,
To live beneath the fountain-well,
With iron bands I bound my heart
For grief that we must live apart.
But now this lady's set you free
And comes with you your queen to be,
My bands of iron have burst asunder.
Let all rejoice to see this wonder!

THE BROTHERS GRIMM

Ali Baba and the Forty Thieves

Kassim and Ali Baba were two brothers who lived in Persia a very long time ago. Their father had left them scarcely anything, but Kassim, having married a woman who had inherited much land and a shop stocked with rich merchandise, became one of the richest merchants in the town. Ali Baba, on the other hand, had married someone just as poor as himself and earned his living as a woodcutter. Loading the wood on to his three asses, his only possessions, he would take it into the town, where he would try to sell it.

One day in the forest Ali Baba noticed a huge cloud of dust rising in the air and approaching in his direction. From the dust cloud there soon emerged a band of horsemen riding at a furious speed. Robbers, thought Ali Baba, and climbing a tree near the foot of a rock he hid himself among its branches. The horsemen, all fully armed, galloped to the rock, where they dismounted. Ali Baba counted forty of them. He was now sure they were robbers; this must be their hideout, where they concealed their booty well away from the town.

They unbridled and tethered their horses and hung hay-bags round the necks of the animals. One man, whom Ali Baba took to be their leader, now approached the rock at the base of the tree where Ali

Baba was hiding and pronounced, very distinctly, two words: 'Open Sesame!' Immediately a door in the rock opened and the chief followed his men inside, after which the door closed. Ali Baba feared to leave his hiding-place lest they might come out again, but after a while the door opened and the thieves emerged. He then heard the chief pronounce the words: 'Shut Sesame' at which the door in the rock closed, each man, laden with a saddle-bag, mounted his horse, and their chief led them off along the route by which they had come. Ali Baba followed them with his eyes till they were out of sight. Then, curious to test the strange words which the chief had used to open and shut the door in the rock, he said, 'Open Sesame' and indeed the door opened wide. As he entered, it closed behind him, and he was amazed to see a beautifully lit, spacious interior with a high ceiling, all seemingly hewn out of the rock by human hands. He beheld vast bales of merchandise, high piles of silk and brocades, precious carpets, but above all veritable mountains of sacks filled with gold and silver. This cave, thought Ali Baba, must have been used for centuries by bandits to store their loot, and he made straight for the gold, removing as many sacks as his asses could carry. When he said 'Open Sesame', and then, 'Shut Sesame', the door in the rock opened and closed behind him and, after loading the sacks on to the asses, he cunningly concealed them under piles of wood. Then he resumed his journey home, stabled his horses, removed the wood covering the sacks, and carried them into the house before the gaze of his astonished wife. He emptied the sacks, which made a great heap of gold, and told his wife of his adventure from beginning to end, with a stern warning to keep it

149

all a dark secret. He would not let her count the coins. 'You will never finish,' he said. 'I shall dig a hole and bury it all. We must lose no time.'

'But,' objected his wife, 'we should at least get some idea of the quantity of money we have. Let me borrow a measuring jar and gauge the value of it while you are digging the hole.' She went off to Kassim's wife and asked to borrow a measuring jar. This woman, fully aware of Ali Baba's poverty, was curious to know what kind of grain was to be measured, so she stuck a small piece of tallow to the bottom end of the jar before giving it to her sister-in-law.

Ali Baba's wife measured all the gold, highly delighted at the number of times she had to fill the jar, and then returned it to Kassim's wife, not noticing that a piece of gold was stuck to the tallow. The moment she left, Kassim's wife examined the measuring jar and was dumbfounded to discover the gold. She was overcome with envy, and as soon as Kassim stepped inside the doorway, she exclaimed, 'So *you* think yourself rich, do you! How wrong you are! Ali Baba is infinitely richer, he doesn't count *coins*, he measures his *gold*.' Kassim demanded an explanation, and she told him what had happened and how, by her own guile, she had made this incredible discovery. She showed him the piece of gold – a coin so old that the name of the monarch stamped on it was unknown to him. Far from being overjoyed at the good fortune that had come his brother's way, he was eaten up with jealousy and scarcely slept that night. Early next morning he burst in upon Ali Baba.

'You pretend to be poor,' he cried, 'yet you measure your gold.'

'Brother,' replied Ali Baba, 'I don't understand what

you are saying.'

But when Kassim showed him the gold stuck to his measuring jar, Ali Baba realized that his secret was out, and he told him how a lucky chance had led him to the treasure cave of a gang of thieves. He even offered to share the treasure if Kassim would keep it all secret.

'That is the very least I would expect,' said Kassim haughtily, 'but if you wish me to keep quiet you must tell me exactly where the treasure is to be found and how I can enter the cave.' Ali Baba, more out of kindness than fear, told him in careful detail all he wished to know, repeating the words which would open and shut the door in the rock.

Kassim left next morning at first light, hungry to seize the treasure for himself before his brother arrived. He took several huge chests on his ten mules, intending to return for more when these were full. He followed the path till he arrived at the tree where Ali Baba had hidden, and soon discovered the door in the rock.

'Open Sesame,' said he and lo, the door opened, Kassim went inside, and the door closed behind him. The riches that met his dazzled eyes were beyond what he could have imagined in his wildest dreams. He proceeded to cram the sacks he had taken into the cave with as much gold as possible, but he was so drunk with excitement and greed that he quite forgot the magic words that opened the door. Instead of 'Open Sesame', he said, 'Open Barley.' To his horror the door did not budge. 'Open Maize,' he cried, with the same result. In vain did he try the name of every grain he could think of – the door remained firmly closed. Panic-stricken, Kassim paced the floor of the cave, but the greater his efforts to recall the magic word, the more 'Sesame' seemed to elude him.

Meanwhile, about noon, the robbers returned and noticed Kassim's mules laden with chests near the door to the cave. The chief dismounted, followed by his men. With sabre in hand he pronounced the magic words, 'Open Sesame', and the door opened.

Locked inside the cave, Kassim had heard the sound of the approaching horsemen. He decided to make a desperate effort to save himself, and the instant the door opened he rushed at the chief and tried with all his strength to force his way out. But the sabres of the other robbers blocked the way, and that was the end of Kassim.

The first concern of the bandits was to search the cave. They then emptied Kassim's sacks but this did not, in any way, provide the answer to the great mystery. They could guess why he had been unable to get out. But how had he got in? They paced the floor and racked their brains, but all in vain. Finally, in case, by some extraordinary means, Kassim had discovered their magic password, they resolved to make an example of his misadventure, as a warning to anyone else who might dare approach their hideout. They hacked his body into quarters and hung them up inside the doorway. Then they mounted their horses and rode away to continue their acts of brigandage on the highway.

Meanwhile Kassim's wife was growing more and more anxious as nightfall approached with still no sign of her husband. In her alarm she ran to Ali Baba, crying, 'Dear brother-in-law, you must have guessed where your brother went this morning. Alas, he is not yet returned. Something terrible must have befallen him.' Ali Baba tried to reassure her by suggesting that

Kassim must have judged it wiser not to return to the town till it was dark enough for his mules to remain unseen. But when by midnight he still failed to appear, her alarm changed to terror. She cursed herself for her greed and envy, which had prompted both her and her husband to intervene in Ali Baba's affairs.

Dawn broke, and Ali Baba was already on his way with his three asses to look for his brother. But there was no sign of either him or his mules. Arriving at the cave, Ali Baba was terrified to see blood trickling from underneath the door. Fearing the worst, he uttered the magic words 'Open Sesame'. The door opened and the hideous sight of his brother's quartered corpse met his horrified gaze. Forgetting his wrongs, he resolved to give Kassim an honourable burial, and having reverently wrapped the parts with some cloth he found in the cave, he loaded them on to an ass, concealing them with pieces of wood. He then hastened back, keeping a watchful eye on his tragic load. He knocked at his sister-in-law's door, which was opened by Morgiana, a shrewd and ingenious slave-girl who could always find a way out of the trickiest situations. Ali Baba took her aside and described the problem, swearing her to secrecy.

'In these two bundles lies the body of your master. We must bury him as though he died a natural death. Now lead me to your mistress.'

'What news of my husband?' cried Kassim's wife, and he told her the sad story, sparing no detail.

'My grief,' he said, 'is no less than yours. But everything must look as though my brother died a natural death. I have instructed Morgiana about this and I assure you she is completely reliable. As for you, dear sister-in-law, you must share fully in our treasure and our home.' Kassim's widow listened in silence and tried to console herself with Ali Baba's generous offer.

Now Morgiana had already worked out a plan. She went to an apothecary and requested him to make up a potion for a very serious illness. 'My poor master, Kassim, is dangerously ill,' she said. 'He can neither eat nor speak.' The following day she went again to the apothecary, and with many a sigh she asked him to prepare a potion for a person who was on the point of death. With a sob in her voice and heaving a great sigh, she said, 'I fear I am about to lose the kindest of masters.'

Meanwhile, Ali Baba and his wife were to be seen coming to and from Kassim's house all day long with sad faces, and at last the neighbours heard the mournful wailings of Morgiana and Kassim's wife. So it came as no surprise when Morgiana announced that Kassim had died.

The next day at sunrise she hurried to a shoemaker of her acquaintance and, putting a coin in his hand, she said, 'Baba Mustapha, get your needle and thread and let me lead you blindfold to a certain place.'

'Are you persuading me to do something dis-honourable?' protested the shoemaker.

'Heaven forbid!' said Morgiana, pressing a further gold coin into his palm. 'Nothing I am asking you to do will tarnish your honour.'

Baba Mustapha then allowed himself to be led blind-fold to the place where she had hidden the four quarters of the body. Having removed the blindfold, she told the startled shoemaker, 'I want you to sew these four pieces together, and then you will receive two more pieces of gold.' When he had completed this gruesome task, she gave him the gold, blindfolded him again and received his undertaking that he would keep the matter a secret. She then led him back to his house.

Ali Baba now arrived, washed the body and sprayed it with incense and, with Morgiana's help, lowered it into the coffin. The usual rites were performed and wailing neighbours followed the coffin to the burial ground. Ali Baba went with them, but Kassim's widow remained in the house grieving and lamenting in the company of other women, as was the custom. Thus the entire neighbourhood mourned the death of Kassim the merchant, and nothing sinister was suspected.

Let us now leave Ali Baba and return to the forty thieves. They came back to their cave and were quite bewildered to find that the quartered body had vanished. 'We've been found out,' said the chief, 'and if we're not careful we shall lose everything. Bit by bit all the wealth of our ancestors, so painfully accumulated over the years, will be snatched from us. There is obviously someone else helping himself to our treasure, and we must devote all our efforts to finding him.'

The robbers then decided that one of them must go into the town disguised as a traveller, listen for any gossip about the bizarre death of the man they had murdered, and find out where he lived. One of the robbers volunteered for the task, offering to die if he failed.

In the town square the only shop open when the disguised traveller walked in at dawn was that of Baba Mustapha, who was busy at work, awl in hand. 'You must have remarkable eyesight to handle the needle in this half-light,' said the bandit to him after exchanging a greeting.

'You obviously do not know me, young man,' replied Baba Mustapha. 'Old as I am, my eyesight is excellent. Only a short while ago I sewed together the parts of a corpse in a place as dark as the one you are in at this moment.'

The robber was overjoyed to receive the very information he was seeking from the first man he asked. 'I do not wish to pry into your secrets,' he said, 'but if you were to show me where exactly you did this remarkable piece of stitching, you would not go unrewarded.'

'This I cannot do,' replied Baba Mustapha, 'for I was led blindfold to the spot.'

'Then let me blindfold you,' said the bandit, 'and let us walk together along the road. This may remind you of the way you went.'

He then pressed a gold coin into the shoemaker's hand and blindfolded him. They began walking, and after a while Baba Mustapha stopped. 'I feel I went no further than this point.' Indeed, they were outside Kassim's house, which was where Ali Baba and his wife also now lived. The bandit marked the house with a cross, removed the blindfold, thanked Baba Mustapha and returned to the forest.

Soon after, Morgiana, returning from some errand, noticed the cross. 'Who could have done that?' she wondered. 'No doubt, someone who wishes to harm my new master.' She then marked several neighbouring doors with crosses, but mentioned nothing of this to Ali Baba.

The robber reported the success of his mission to his chief, who now split his gang into small groups and told them to meet at the house marked with a cross, where he and the triumphant robber would be waiting. The robber's humiliation and his chief's fury may well be imagined when they found that several houses had been marked. The cross made by the robber was in no way different from all the other crosses, and the plan was a failure. The chief ordered his men to return to their hideout, and the unsuccessful bandit accepted his fate and was beheaded.

The following day the scheme was tried once more by a second volunteer who, this time, marked the house with a red cross. But Morgiana's eagle eye saw it and she marked the surrounding houses with red crosses. And so the second bandit failed in his mission and was beheaded accordingly.

The chief now resolved that he himself would seek out Baba Mustapha and find that elusive house once and for all. Having been conducted there by the shoemaker, he spent several minutes inspecting every single detail of the house and memorized them – but without marking it in any way. Returning to his men, he assured them that they were now in a position to take full revenge on the scoundrel who had penetrated their lair. 'I am certain of the correct house,' he said, 'and if you follow my plan we will soon rid ourselves of this enemy. But first we must procure nineteen mules and thirty-eight large leathern oil jars. One of these will be filled with oil, and the others left empty.'

The men set about procuring the mules and oil jars and when all was ready the chief put each man, fully armed, into a jar and, leaving only sufficient opening for breathing, securely clamped down the lids and smeared oil all over the outsides to give the impression that each jar was really filled with oil. He then led them towards the town, reaching Ali Baba's house by dusk. He found the master of the house taking the air by the open front door, and addressed him: 'Good sir, I am an oil merchant, as you can see, and have journeyed far to sell my oil in the market here tomorrow. It is late, and I fear I may not find a place to spend the night. I should be most grateful if, in your generosity, you could spare a night's lodging space for me and my mules.'

Now although Ali Baba had seen this man in the forest and had even heard his voice, he did not recognize him, cunningly disguised as he was. 'You are most welcome,' he replied. 'Pray enter, my home is at your disposal.' He made way for the mules to pass into his courtyard, where a slave was ordered to stable them and unburden them of their load of 'oil jars'. He bade Morgiana prepare a meal for his guest and a comfortable bed for him to spend the night. He welcomed him into the spacious hall which was reserved for important visitors and regaled him with a veritable banquet. When they had eaten, the chief requested that he might inspect his mules to make sure they were in condition for travel the next day. His true intention, however, was to give his men hidden in the jars instructions for their part in his plot. Starting with the first jar and continuing till he reached the last, he said to each bandit, 'When I throw a few small stones from my bedroom window to hit your jar, you must force the jar open and jump out. I shall join you straight away.' He then returned to the house, where Morgiana conducted him to his room by candlelight. But he did not undress, so that he might be ready immediately the right moment came.

Morgiana, with her fellow slave Abdulla, now

busied herself preparing their master's linen for the next day and making the soup for the midday meal. Just as Abdulla was skimming the soup, the lamp went out. Finding they were out of both oil and candles, they were at a loss. What was to be done? Then Morgiana remembered the oil in the jars in the stable. Out she sallied with a jug. Imagine her surprise when she heard a voice whispering from the first jar, 'Is it time?' The voice came quite clearly through the small opening which allowed the bandit to breathe. The astute Morgiana was quick to grasp what was going on; there must be a man concealed in the jar. Pretending to be the chief, she whispered back, 'Not yet, but soon.' The same thing happened with all the remaining jars, except, of course, the last one, which was filled with oil. 'Great Allah,' Morgiana thought, 'thirty-seven thieves concealed in jars in our court-yard, and their chief treated as a guest in our house!' She filled her jug with oil from the last jar, returned to the kitchen, filled the lamp and lit it. She then took a cauldron, went out and filled it with oil, and placed it on a fire which she stoked up with plenty of wood. When the oil was boiling she took a jug of it and poured enough into each jar to kill the villains inside; for this she had to make several journeys to and from the kitchen, but she did it almost noiselessly. Then she damped down the fire somewhat, and put out the lamp. But she did not go to bed. She was anxious to see what would happen next.

It was not long before the chief got up and, judging by the silence that the household was deep in sleep, gave the agreed signal to his men by throwing little stones at the jars from his bedroom window. He got no response, however carefully he listened. Nor was there any movement, though he continued throwing stones. He came down in a state of great alarm, entered the courtyard and discovered the truth; not one of his men had escaped. In complete despair he fled through the garden, abandoning his mules, and when Morgiana saw that he had gone she heaved a deep sigh of relief and satisfaction in the knowledge that the family were now safe from harm.

Ali Baba, knowing nothing of the night's events, was astonished next morning to find the oil jars still standing in the courtyard, the merchant vanished and the mules all there. He asked Morgiana what this was all about.

'My good master,' she said, 'it was the will of Allah that you and your family should be saved. You will understand better what has taken place when I have shown you all that is to be seen.

'Look into the jar,' she said as Ali Baba followed her into the courtyard, 'and tell me if you see any oil in it.' Ali Baba obeyed her and was horrified at what he saw. 'There is a dead thief in each of these jars,' said Morgiana, 'but you must suppress your astonishment and horror lest we arouse the curiosity of our neighbours.' She then explained how she had used the oil from the single oil jar to put an end to her master's would-be assassins. Ali Baba stood speechless, rooted to the spot. 'But the merchant,' he managed to mutter at last, 'what has become of him?'

'He has made his escape and left his mules behind,' she replied, and she told him how her suspicions had first been aroused by the sight of a white cross on their door, and how she confused the robbers by marking all the other doors. 'And now, master, I beg of you to be on your guard,' she concluded. 'As for me, I shall continue to watch over you, as is my duty.'

So overwhelmed was Ali Baba by the loyalty of Morgiana, who had saved the lives of them all, that he, there and then, granted her her freedom. 'But, I beseech you, remain with us as one of our household.' Then together they buried all the robbers and the jars in a deep pit at the bottom of Ali Baba's vast gardens, while the mules were sold off one by one.

The robber chief returned to his cave mortified and humiliated, burning with an even fiercer desire for revenge. The next day he disguised himself and went into the town, where he took up lodgings and inquired of the landlady whether anything untoward had happened thereabouts recently. She told him of this and that but said nothing relating to the events he was concerned with. The chief realized that Ali Baba must have kept the matter secret, just as he had done with Kassim's quartered body. He furnished his lodgings with the finest merchandise from his treasure cave, and then set himself up in a handsome store opposite the warehouse which had been Kassim's but which Ali Baba had presented to his own son on his uncle's death. He assumed the name of Cogia Hussein and soon made friends with the merchants around, particularly with Ali Baba's son, whom he frequently invited to dine, and soon called his closest friend. The son dearly wished to return Cogia's lavish hospitality but felt that his home was not rich enough to receive him. Ali Baba was only too happy to entertain this good man on his son's behalf. 'Tomorrow,' he told his son, 'after you have taken your walk with Cogia Hussein, pretend you are just making a call at my house. I shall ask Morgiana to prepare a lavish repast.'

And so, the following day, as they were nearing Ali Baba's house, his son asked his friend if he would do his respected father the honour of calling upon him. This, of couse, was just what the robber chief had been waiting for. With a bow he accepted.

Ali Baba gave Cogia Hussein a gracious welcome, thanking him for all he had done for his son. He then humbly invited him to dine with them, though the meal, he declared, would be as nothing compared with what Cogia Hussein deserved. 'But such as it is,' he said, 'I offer it with my full heart.'

'Sir,' said Hussein, 'of the goodness of your heart I have no doubt, but pray think no ill of me if I do not accept your generous offer. I eat no meat nor any dish containing salt. I would therefore feel out of place at your table.'

'If that be the case, have no fear. No salt shall be put in any of your dishes.'

When Ali Baba went to the kitchen to tell Morgiana to refrain from putting salt in the guest's dishes, her curiosity was aroused.

'Who is this guest?' she asked. 'Is it not written that he who will not eat salt at your table can be no friend?'

'He is an honest man,' Ali Baba reassured her, 'have no fear.' But at the very first glimpse of the guest, and despite his cunning disguise, Morgiana was in no doubt that this man was the robber chief, and on approaching more closely as she set down his dish, she observed that there was a dagger concealed under his robe.

'He is my master's sworn enemy,' she murmured to herself. 'He intends to murder him, but I will never let that happen.'

Morgiana continued to serve the meal and the dessert fruits, after which she placed three goblets of wine next to her master. 'This is the moment,' thought the guest, 'most favourable for my purposes. When father and son have drunk their fill, they will observe nothing, and I can put an end to them both with my dagger and escape through the garden as before.'

But he reckoned without the shrewd Morgiana. She went to her room and dressed herself as a dancer, and in a jewelled girdle round her waist she concealed a small silver dagger. To complete her disguise she put on a mask, told Abdulla to fetch his tambourine, and entered the dining hall, ready to entertain the company.

Abdulla began to play upon his tambourine, and Morgiana, bowing low, began to dance. The robber chief had not expected this diversion, and he feared he might lose the opportunity to execute his plan, but he continued his pretence of friendliness to his host. Morgiana's dancing was beautiful, and her unexpected darting and withdrawing movements made her performance extremely exciting. Suddenly and startlingly, she threw herself forward, at the same time drawing her dagger as though this were a part of her dance, and pointing it at her own bosom. Finally, quite breathless, she signed to Abdulla to cease playing while she took the tambourine and offered it to Ali Baba as a token of respect. Then she stepped towards Cogia Hussein and as he drew a few coins from under his robe to throw to her, she plunged the dagger deep into his chest.

Ali Baba and his son let out a cry of horror.

'Wretched girl, what have you done?' they cried. 'What dishonour have you brought upon our family!'

'What I have done was not to dishonour you or your family,' answered Morgiana, 'but to preserve all your lives,' and pulling open the robber's robe she revealed his hidden dagger.

'This is the villainous guest that you have been entertaining,' she continued, 'none other than the chief of the robbers himself. Now you can understand why he would eat no salt at your table. And it was that which aroused my suspicions.'

Thus for the second time did Morgiana save the life of Ali Baba. He was overwhelmed with gratitude and embraced her, saying, 'Oh dear Morgiana, I have already given you your liberty. Will you now honour both me and my son by agreeing to become his wife?'

Morgiana was extremely happy to accept, and Ali Baba's son was overjoyed, for he found her most pleasing in every respect.

The last of the robbers was buried in the same secret place as the others, and a few weeks later the marriage of Ali Baba's son to Morgiana was celebrated with great solemnity and sumptuous feasting, dancing and rejoicing of every kind.

After a year or so had passed Ali Baba was seized with curiosity to see the treasure cave again. When he arrived at the rock, he approached with caution, for he did not know that all the forty thieves were dead: there had been only thirty-seven in the thirty-seven oil jars and no one knew what had become of the two bandits who had been beheaded.

But when Ali Baba pronounced, 'Open Sesame', he was in fact the only man in the entire world who knew these magic words. He filled his chests with gold and returned to his home.

Ali Baba passed on the secret of the treasure cave to his son, and he in turn to his children, and so on from generation to generation.

from THE ARABIAN NIGHTS

Rumpelstiltskin

There was once a poor miller who had a beautiful daughter. Now it happened that he had occasion to speak with the king, and in order to give himself an air of importance he said to him, 'I have a daughter who can spin straw into gold.' The king said to the miller, 'Now that is an art which pleases me greatly. If your daughter is as skilled as you claim, bring her to my castle tomorrow and I will put her to the test.' When the girl was brought to him, he led her into a room which was filled with straw, gave her a wheel and bobbin, and said, 'Now get to work, and if you have not spun this straw into gold by morning, then you must die.' And then he locked the door of the room and she was left alone inside.

And so there sat the poor miller's daughter, not knowing what on earth to do. She had no idea at all how to spin straw into gold, and as her fear grew greater and greater she began to weep. Suddenly the door opened, and a tiny little man stepped in and said, 'Good evening to you, miller maiden, why do you weep so bitterly?' 'Ah!' replied the girl, 'I am to spin this straw into gold and am at a loss how to do it.' Then the little man said, 'What will you give me if I do it for you?'

'My necklace,' said the girl. The little man took the necklace, sat himself down in front of the little wheel and, whirr, whirr, whirr, three times round, and the bobbin was full. Then he put another one on and whirr, whirr, whirr, three times round, and the second one was full. And so it went on like that till morning, and all the straw was spun and all the bobbins were full of gold. At sunrise the king appeared, and when he saw the gold he was astonished and overjoyed, but his heart only became all the greedier for more.

That night he had the miller's daughter taken into another room full of straw which was even larger than the first room and commanded her to spin it all in one night, if she valued her life. The girl had no idea what to do and began to weep. Suddenly the door flew open once again, and the tiny little man appeared and said, 'What will you give me if I spin this straw into gold?' 'This ring on my finger,' replied the girl. The little man took the ring, began once more whirring the wheel and by morning had spun all the straw into gleaming gold.

The king's joy knew no bounds when he saw this, but his hunger for gold was still not satisfied. The girl was led into another, even bigger, room full of straw, and the king told her, 'You must spin all this tonight and if you succeed you will be my wife.' 'Even though she is only a miller's daughter,' he thought to himself, 'I shall not find a richer wife than this one in the whole wide world.'

When the girl was alone again the little man returned a third time and said, 'What will you give me if I spin the straw again for you?'

'I have nothing else that I can give you,' answered the girl.

'Well then, promise to give me your first child when you become queen.'

'Who knows how things will go?' thought the miller's daughter, and in her distress she could think of no other way out, so she promised the little man what he asked and in return he once more spun the straw into gold. And when the king came in the morning and found that everything had gone as he wished, he married the girl, and so the miller's daughter became a queen.

At the end of a year she gave birth to a beautiful child. She had forgotten all about the little man, but suddenly one night he stepped into her room and said, 'Now give me what you promised.'

The queen was terrorstruck and offered him all the wealth of the kingdom if only he would let her keep her child. But the little man said, 'No, I prefer something living to all the treasure in the world.'

Then the queen set up such a crying and wailing that he took pity on her. 'I will give you three days,' he said. 'If in that time you find out my name, you may keep the child.'

All night long the queen racked her brains, thinking of every name she had ever heard, and then she sent a messenger travelling throughout the land to make inquiries far and wide about all possible names.

When the little man arrived the next day she began with Caspar, Melchior, Balthazar, and all the other names that she knew, one after the other, but after each one the little man said, 'No, that's not my name.' The second day she sent messengers to ask all around what people's names were, and she offered the little man the most unusual and oddest of names.

'Is your name perhaps Beefyribs or Sheepyshank or Ropesleg?' But each time the answer came, 'No, that's not my name.'

On the third day the first messenger came back and informed the queen, 'I have not found a single new name, but when I came to a high mountain on the outskirts of the forest, where fox and hare are good neighbours, I espied there a small house, and in front of the house there was a fire burning, and round this fire there was a most ridiculous little man, hopping on one leg and singing:

> *Merrily the feast I'll make,*
> *Today I'll brew, tomorrow bake,*
> *Merrily I dance and sing*
> *For this day will a stranger bring.*
> *Little can she guess, poor dame,*
> *That Rumpelstiltskin is my name.*

You can imagine how overjoyed the queen was when she heard that name. And when, soon after, the little man appeared and said, 'Now, Lady Queen, what is my name?' she first asked, 'Is your name Bandyfiggle?'

'No.'

'Is your name Fishface?'

'No.'

'Is your name Rumpelstiltskin?'

'The devil told you! The devil told you!' shrieked the little man, and in his fury he thrust his right foot so deep into the ground that he sank right up to his waist. Then in his rage he grabbed hold of his left foot and with both hands tore himself in two.

THE BROTHERS GRIMM

Jack and the Beanstalk

There was once upon a time a poor widow who had an only son named Jack, and a cow named Milky-white. And all they had to live on was the milk the cow gave every morning, which they carried to the market and sold. But one morning Milky-white gave no milk, and they didn't know what to do.

'What shall we do, what shall we do?' said the widow, wringing her hands.

'Cheer up, mother, I'll go and get work somewhere,' said Jack.

'We've tried that before, and nobody would take you,' said his mother. 'We must sell Milky-white and with the money start a shop, or something.'

'All right, mother,' says Jack. 'It's market-day today, and I'll soon sell Milky-white, and then we'll see what we can do.'

So he took the cow's halter in his hand, and off he started. He hadn't gone far when he met a funny-looking old man, who said to him: 'Good morning, Jack.'

'Good morning to you,' said Jack, and wondered how he knew his name.

'Well, Jack, and where are you off to?' said the man.

'I'm going to market to sell our cow here.'

'Oh, you look the proper sort of chap to sell cows,' said the man. 'I wonder if you know how many beans make five.'

'Two in each hand and one in your mouth,' says Jack, as sharp as a needle.

'Right you are,' says the man, 'and here they are, the very beans themselves,' he went on, pulling out of his pocket a number of strange-looking beans. 'As you are so sharp,' says he, 'I don't mind doing a swop with you – your cow for these beans.'

'Go along,' says Jack; 'wouldn't you like it!'

'Ah! you don't know what these beans are,' said the man. 'If you plant them overnight, by morning they grow right up to the sky.'

'Really?' said Jack. 'You don't say so.'

'Yes, that is so, and if it doesn't turn out to be true you can have your cow back.'

'Right,' says Jack, and hands him over Milky-white's halter and pockets the beans.

Back goes Jack home, and as he hadn't gone very far it wasn't dusk by the time he got to his door.

'Back already, Jack?' said his mother. 'I see you haven't got Milky-white, so you've sold her. How much did you get for her?'

'You'll never guess, mother,' says Jack.

'No, you don't say so. Good boy! Five pounds, ten, fifteen, no, it can't be twenty.'

'I told you you couldn't guess. What do you say to these beans; they're magical, plant them overnight and – '

'What!' says Jack's mother, 'have you been such a fool, such a dolt, such an idiot, as to give away my Milky-white, the best milker in the parish, and prime beef to boot, for a set of paltry beans? Take that! Take that! Take that! And as for your precious beans, here they go out of the window. And now off with you to bed. Not a sup shall you drink, and not a bit shall you

171

swallow this very night.'

So Jack went upstairs to his little room in the attic, and sad and sorry he was, to be sure, as much for his mother's sake, as for the loss of his supper.

At last he dropped off to sleep.

When he woke up, the room looked so funny. The sun was shining into part of it, and yet all the rest was quite dark and shady. So Jack jumped up and dressed himself and went to the window. And what do you think he saw? Why, the beans his mother had thrown out of the window into the garden had sprung up into a big beanstalk which went up and up and up till it reached the sky. So the man spoke truth after all.

The beanstalk grew up quite close past Jack's window, so all he had to do was to open it and give a jump on to the beanstalk, which ran up just like a big ladder. So Jack climbed, and he climbed and he climbed and he climbed and he climbed and he climbed and he climbed till at last he reached the sky. And when he got there he found a long broad road going as straight as a dart. So he walked along and he walked along and he walked along till he came to a great big tall house, and on the doorstep there was a great big tall woman.

'Good morning, mum,' says Jack, quite polite-like. 'Could you be so kind as to give me some breakfast?' For he hadn't had anything to eat, you know, the night before, and was as hungry as a hunter.

'It's breakfast you want, is it?' says the great big tall woman, 'it's breakfast you'll be if you don't move off from here. My man is an ogre and there's nothing he likes better than boys broiled on toast. You'd better be moving on or he'll soon be coming.'

'Oh! please, mum, do give me something to eat, mum. I've had nothing to eat since yesterday morning, really and truly, mum,' says Jack. 'I may as well be broiled as die of hunger.'

Well, the ogre's wife was not half so bad after all. So she took Jack into the kitchen, and gave him a hunk of bread and cheese and a jug of milk. But Jack hadn't half finished these when thump! thump! thump! the whole house began to tremble with the noise of someone coming.

'Good gracious me! It's my old man,' said the ogre's wife, 'what on earth shall I do? Come along quick and jump in here.' And she bundled Jack into the oven just as the ogre came in.

He was a big one, to be sure. At his belt he had three calves strung up by the heels, and he unhooked them and threw them down on the table and said: 'Here, wife, broil me a couple of these for breakfast. Ah! what's this I smell?

> *Fee-fi-fo-fum,*
> *I smell the blood of an Englishman,*
> *Be he alive, or be he dead*
> *I'll have his bones to grind my bread.*

'Nonsense, dear,' said his wife, 'you're dreaming. Or perhaps you smell the scraps of that little boy you liked so much for yesterday's dinner. Here, you go and have a wash and tidy up, and by the time you come back your breakfast'll be ready for you.'

So off the ogre went, and Jack was just going to jump out of the oven and run away when the woman told him not. 'Wait till he's asleep,' says she. 'He always has a doze after breakfast.'

Well, the ogre had his breakfast, and after that he goes to a big chest and takes out of it a couple of bags of gold, and down he sits and counts till at last his head began to nod and he began to snore till the whole house shook again.

Then Jack crept out on tiptoe from his oven, and as he was passing the ogre he took one of the bags of gold under his arm, and off he pelters till he came to the beanstalk, and then he threw down the bag of gold, which, of course, fell into his mother's garden, and then he climbed down and climbed down till at last he got home and told his mother and showed her the gold and said: 'Well, mother, wasn't I right about the beans? They are really magical, you see.'

So they lived on the bag of gold for some time, but at last they came to the end of it, and Jack made up his mind to try his luck once more at the top of the beanstalk. So one fine morning he rose up early, and got on to the beanstalk, and he climbed and he climbed and he climbed and he climbed and he climbed and he climbed till at last he came out on to the road again and up to the great big tall house he had been to before. There, sure enough, was the great big tall woman standing on the doorstep.

'Good morning, mum,' says Jack, as bold as brass, 'could you be so good as to give me something to eat?'

'Go away, my boy,' said the big tall woman, 'or else my man will eat you up for breakfast. But aren't you the youngster who came here once before? Do you know, that very day my man missed one of his bags of gold.'

'That's strange, mum,' said Jack, 'I dare say I could tell you something about that, but I'm so hungry I can't speak till I've had something to eat.'

Well, the big tall woman was so curious that she took him in and gave him something to eat. But he had scarcely begun munching it as slowly as he could when thump! thump! they heard the giant's footsteps, and his wife hid Jack away in the oven.

All happened as it did before. In came the ogre as he did before, said: 'Fee-fi-fo-fum', and had his breakfast of three broiled oxen. Then he said: 'Wife, bring me the hen that lays the golden eggs.' So she brought it, and the ogre said: 'Lay', and it laid an egg of gold. And then the ogre began to nod his head, and to snore till the house shook.

Then Jack crept out of the oven on tiptoe and caught hold of the golden hen, and was off before you could say 'Jack Robinson'. But this time the hen gave a cackle which woke the ogre, and just as Jack got out of the house he heard him calling: 'Wife, wife, what have you done with my golden hen?'

And the wife said: 'Why, my dear?'

But that was all Jack heard, for he rushed off to the beanstalk and climbed down like a house on fire. And when he got home he showed his mother the wonderful hen, and said, 'Lay' to it; and it laid a golden egg every time he said, 'Lay'.

Well, Jack was not content, and it wasn't very long before he determined to have another try at his luck up there at the top of the beanstalk. So one fine morning, he rose up early, and got on to the beanstalk, and he climbed and he climbed and he climbed and he climbed till he got to the top. But this time he knew better than to go straight to the ogre's house. And when he got near it, he waited behind a bush till he saw the ogre's wife come out with a pail to get some water, and then he crept into the house and got into the copper. He hadn't been there long when he heard thump! thump! thump! as before, and in came the ogre and his wife.

'Fee-fi-fo-fum, I smell the blood of an Englishman,' cried out the ogre. 'I smell him, wife, I smell him.'

'Do you, my dearie?' says the ogre's wife. 'Then, if it's that little rogue that stole your gold and the hen that laid the golden eggs, he's sure to have got into the oven.' And they both rushed to the oven. But Jack wasn't there, luckily, and the ogre's wife said: 'There you are again with your fee-fi-fo-fum. Why, of course, it's the boy you caught last night that I've just broiled for your breakfast. How forgetful I am, and how careless you are not to know the difference between live and dead after all these years.'

So the ogre sat down to the breakfast and ate it, but every now and then he would mutter: 'Well, I could have sworn – ' and he'd get up and search the larder and the cupboards and everything, only, luckily, he didn't think of the copper.

After breakfast was over, the ogre called out: 'Wife, wife, bring me my golden harp.' So she brought it and put it on the table before him. Then he said: 'Sing!' and the golden harp sang most beautifully. And it went on singing till the ogre fell asleep, and commenced to snore like thunder.

Then Jack lifted up the copper-lid very quietly and got down like a mouse and crept on hands and knees till he came to the table, when up he crawled, caught hold of the golden harp and dashed with it towards the door. But the harp called out quite loud: 'Master! Master!' and the ogre woke up just in time to see Jack running off with his harp.

Jack ran as fast as he could, and the ogre came rushing after, and would soon have caught him only Jack had a start and dodged him a bit and knew where he was going. When he got to the beanstalk the ogre was not more than twenty yards away when suddenly he saw Jack disappear like, and when he came to the end of the road he saw Jack underneath climbing down for dear life. Well, the ogre didn't like trusting himself to such a ladder, and he stood and waited, so Jack got another start. But just then the harp cried out: 'Master! Master!' and the ogre swung himself down on to the beanstalk, which shook with his weight. Down climbs Jack, and after him climbed the ogre. By this time Jack had climbed down and climbed down and climbed down till he was very nearly home. So he called out: 'Mother! Mother! Bring me an axe, bring me an axe.' And his mother came rushing out with the axe in her hand, but when she came to the beanstalk she stood stock still with fright, for there she saw the ogre with his legs just through the clouds.

But Jack jumped down and got hold of the axe and gave a chop at the beanstalk which cut it half in two. The ogre felt the beanstalk shake and quiver, so he stopped to see what was the matter. Then Jack gave another chop with the axe, and the beanstalk was cut in two and began to topple over. Then the ogre fell down and broke his crown, and the beanstalk came toppling after.

Then Jack showed his mother his golden harp, and what with showing that and selling the golden eggs, Jack and his mother became very rich, and he married a great princess, and they lived happy ever after.

JOSEPH JACOBS

The Story of the Three Bears

To my dear children, Maja, Harry, and Herbert:

The 'Story of the Three Bears' is a very old nursery tale, but it was never so well told as by the great poet Southey, whose version I have (with permission) given you, only I have made the intruder a little girl instead of an old woman. This I did because I found that the tale is better known with Silver-hair,* and because there are so many other stories of old women.

Your Loving father J. C.
Kentish Town
Nov. 1849.

*We have changed her name to Goldilocks because we all know her by that name today. S. and S. C.

Once upon a time there were Three Bears, who lived together in a house of their own, in a wood. One of them was a Little, Small, Wee Bear; and one was a Middle-sized Bear; and the other was a Great, Huge Bear. They had each a pot for their porridge: a little pot for the Little, Small, Wee Bear; and a middle-sized pot for the Middle Bear; and a great pot for the Great, Huge Bear. And they had each a chair to sit in: a little chair for the Little, Small, Wee Bear; and a middle-sized chair for the Middle Bear; and a great chair for the Great, Huge Bear. And they had each a bed to sleep in: a little bed for the Little, Small, Wee Bear; a middle-sized bed for the Middle Bear; and a great bed for the Great, Huge Bear.

One day, after they had made the porridge for their breakfast, and poured it into their porridge pots, they walked out into the wood while the porridge was cooling, that they might not burn their mouths by beginning too soon to eat it. And while they were walking, a little girl named Goldilocks came into the house. First she looked in at the window, and then she peeped in at the key-hole; and seeing nobody in the house, she lifted the latch. The door was not fastened, because the Bears were good Bears, who did nobody any harm, and never suspected that anybody would harm them. So little Goldilocks opened the door, and went in; and well pleased she was when she saw the porridge on the table. If she had been a good little girl, she would have waited till the Bears came home, and then, perhaps, they would have asked her to breakfast; for they were good Bears – a little rough or so, as the manner of Bears is, but for all that very good-natured and hospitable.

So first she tasted the porridge of the Great, Huge Bear, and that was too hot for her. And then she tasted the porridge of the Middle Bear and that was too cold for her. And then she went to the porridge of the Little, Small, Wee Bear, and tasted that; and that was neither too hot nor too cold, but just right; and she liked it so well, that she ate it all up.

Then little Goldilocks sat down in the chair of the Great, Huge Bear and that was too hard for her. And then she sat down in the chair of the Middle Bear, and that was too soft for her. And then she sat down in the chair of the Little, Small, Wee Bear, and that was neither too hard nor too soft, but just right. So she

seated herself in it, and there she sat till the bottom of
the chair came out, and down came hers, plump upon
the ground.

Then little Goldilocks went upstairs into the bed-
chamber in which the Three Bears slept. And first she
lay down upon the bed of the Great, Huge Bear; but
that was too high at the head for her. And next she lay
down upon the bed of the Middle Bear; and that was
too high at the foot for her. And then she lay down
upon the bed of the Little, Small, Wee Bear; and that
was neither too high at the head nor at the foot, but
just right. So she covered herself up comfortably, and
lay there till she fell fast asleep.

By this time the Three Bears thought their porridge
would be cool enough; so they came home to
breakfast. And little Goldilocks had left the spoon of
the Great, Huge Bear standing in his porridge.

'Somebody has been at my porridge!'

said the Great, Huge Bear in his great, rough, gruff
voice. And when the Middle Bear looked at hers, she
saw that the spoon was standing in it too.

'Somebody has been at my porridge!'
said the Middle Bear in her middle voice.

Then the Little, Small, Wee Bear looked at his, and
there was the spoon in the porridge-pot, but the porridge was all gone.

'Somebody has been at my porridge and has eaten it all up!'
said the Little, Small, Wee Bear in his little, small, wee
voice.

Upon this the Three Bears, seeing that someone had
entered their house and eaten up the Little, Small,
Wee Bear's breakfast, began to look about them. Now
little Goldilocks had not put the hard cushion straight

when she rose from the chair of the Great, Huge Bear.

'Somebody has been sitting in my chair!'

said the Great, Huge Bear in his great, rough, gruff voice.

And little Goldilocks had squatted down the soft cushion of the Middle Bear.

'Somebody has been sitting in my chair!'
said the Middle Bear in her middle voice.

And you know what little Goldilocks had done to the third chair.

'Somebody has been sitting in my chair and has sat the bottom out of it!'
said the Little, Small, Wee Bear in his little, small, wee voice.

Then the Three Bears thought it necessary that they should make further search; so they went upstairs to their bedchamber. Now little Goldilocks had pulled the pillow of the Great, Huge Bear out of its place.

'Somebody has been lying in my bed!'

said the Great, Huge Bear in his great, rough, gruff voice.

And little Goldilocks had pulled the bolster of the Middle Bear out of its place.

'Somebody has been lying in my bed!'
said the Middle Bear in her middle voice.

And when the Little, Small, Wee Bear came to look at his bed, there was the bolster in its place; and the pillow in its place upon the bolster; and upon the pillow was little Goldilocks's pretty head – which was not in its place, for she had no business there.

'Somebody is lying in my bed – and here she is!'
said the Little, Small, Wee Bear in his little, small, wee voice.

182

Little Goldilocks had heard, in her sleep, the great, rough, gruff voice of the Great, Huge Bear; but she was so fast asleep that it was no more to her than the roaring of wind or the rumbling of thunder. And she had heard the middle voice of the Middle Bear, but it was only as if she had heard someone speaking in a dream. But when she heard the voice of the Little, Small, Wee bear, it was so sharp, so shrill, that it awakened her at once. Up she started; and when she saw the Three Bears on one side of the bed, she tumbled out at the other, and ran to the window. Now the window was open, because the Bears, like good, tidy bears, as they were, always opened their bed-chamber window when they got up in the morning. Out little Goldilocks jumped; and away she ran into the woods, and the Three Bears never saw anything more of her.

ROBERT SOUTHEY

John Cundall published the present version of *The Three Bears* (i.e., the version we are all familiar with) in a volume entitled *A Treasury of Pleasure Books for Young Children* in 1850. He used the poet Robert Southey's text, published in 1837 as 'The Story of the Three Bears', and, with his permission, replaced the cantankerous old lady (of Southey's tale) by a little girl whom he styled Silver-Hair. With the passage of time she has become Goldilocks.

Bluebeard

Once upon a time there lived a man who owned beautiful houses both in town and in the country. His dishes were of gold and silver, his furniture was lavishly embroidered, and he rode in gilded carriages. But unfortunately this man had a blue beard, which made him so ugly that there wasn't a woman or girl who didn't run away at the sight of him.

One of his neighbours, a lady of high birth, had two outstandingly beautiful daughters. He wished to marry one of them, but left it to the lady to decide which one she would choose for him. Neither of the daughters was willing to have him, and they kept sending him back and forth, from one to the other, quite unable to bring themselves to accept a man with a blue beard. And what put them off even more was that he had already married several women, and no one knew what had become of them.

So that he and the two daughters should become better acquainted, Bluebeard took them and their mother, with three or four of their best friends and a few other young people of the neighbourhood, to one of his country houses, where they stayed for a full week. The whole time was spent in hunting and fishing parties, walks in the countryside, dances and parties and hearty eating. No one seemed to go to bed; the whole night was spent in playing merry pranks. In short, the younger daughter began to find that the master of the house had a beard that was not so very blue after all and that he was really a man of culture and good taste. No sooner were they back in town than the marriage was celebrated.

After a month had elapsed, Bluebeard informed his wife that he had to make a journey out into the provinces on a matter of considerable importance and that he would be away for at least six weeks. He begged her to enjoy herself while he was absent; to invite her close friends; to take them to his country house if she so desired; and to live in style both in town and in the country.

'Here,' he told her, 'are the keys of the two great rooms with my richest furniture. This one is for the gold and silver dishes which are not in everyday use, and these are for the strong-boxes, which contain all my money and my gold and silver. These are the keys of my jewel caskets. And finally, here is the master key to all the apartments. But as to this small key, it is the key to the little room at the end of the great gallery on the ground floor. You may open everything and go everywhere, but as regards the little room, I forbid you to open it. In fact, I forbid it so strictly that if you so much as opened the door, I warn you that my anger would be beyond anything you might expect.' She promised to obey his orders to the last detail and so, having embraced her, he got into his carriage and set out on his journey.

Her close friends and neighbours did not wait for an invitation to go and visit the young bride, so impatient were they to cast their eyes on all the riches of the house, for they had not dared to come while the husband was there, so great was their fear of his blue

beard. And so there they were, wandering through
the rooms, peering at the chests and wardrobes, each
more rich and sumptuous than the next. They then
proceeded to the rooms where the fine furniture was
stored, and they were almost speechless in their
admiration for the number and beauty of the
tapestries, the beds, the sofas, the closets, the
occasional tables and the large tables, and the mirrors
which afforded them a full view of themselves from
head to foot; some had frames of glass, others of silver
or gilded silver – the most beautiful and magnificent
that they had ever set eyes on. Loud were their
praises, and they never stopped expressing their envy
of their friend's happiness. But she, in the meantime,
felt little pleasure at seeing all this wealth, for she was
bursting with impatience to go and open the little
room on the ground floor.

So pressing indeed was her curiosity that, forgetting
her good manners, she left her companions and went
down by a hidden staircase and with such haste that
twice or thrice she nearly broke her neck. But when
she was actually at the door of the little room, she
paused a while, remembering how strictly her husband had forbidden her and pondering on the
unhappy fate which might befall her were she to be
disobedient. But the temptation was so strong that she
could not resist it. She took the small key and with
trembling hand opened the door of the little room. At
first she saw nothing, for the windows were shut-
tered, but after a few moments, when her eyes had
adjusted to the dark, she saw that the floor was
covered with clotted blood, in which were mirrored
the corpses of several women laid out along the walls.
These were all the wives Bluebeard had married and

whose throats he had cut, one after another. She thought she would die of fright and the key, which she had withdrawn from the lock, fell from her hand. After regaining her presence of mind a little, she picked up the key, locked the door and went back up to her room to try to recover from the shock. But this was beyond her powers, the sight had been too much for her. She noticed that the key to the room was stained with blood, and she made two or three attempts to remove it, but the blood would not go away. In vain did she try to wash it off and even to scour it with fine sand and soap – the blood stayed where it was, for the key was magic and there was no means of rubbing away the stain completely; when the blood was removed from one side of the key it would reappear on the other side.

Bluebeard returned from his journey that very evening, saying he had received letters while on his way, informing him that the matter for which he had set out had been settled to his advantage. His wife did her best to convince him that she was overjoyed at his early return. The following day he asked her to give back the keys to him. She did so, but with a hand so shaky that he guessed straight away what had happened.

'How is it,' he asked, 'that the key to the little room is not with the other keys?'

'I must have left it upstairs on my table,' she replied.

'Be sure that you give it back to me very soon,' said Bluebeard.

She tried to delay for as long as she could, but finally she had no choice but to bring the key back to him.

'Why is there blood on this key?' asked Bluebeard, after considering it for some time.

'I know nothing of that,' replied the wretched woman, pale as death.

'You know nothing of it!' said Bluebeard. 'Well, *I* know. You wanted to open the door of the little room, didn't you? Very well, madam, you will open it and go inside and take your place beside those other ladies you saw there.'

She threw herself at her husband's feet, beseeching him to pardon her and showing all the signs of true repentance for having disobeyed him. She was so beautiful and crestfallen, she would have moved a heart of stone. But Bluebeard had a heart harder than any stone.

'You must die, madam,' he said, 'and soon.'

'Since I must die,' she said, her eyes bathed in tears, 'allow me just a brief time to say my prayers.'

'I grant you a quarter of an hour,' said Bluebeard, 'but not one moment more.'

When she was alone she called out to her sister. 'Sister Anne,' she said to her, 'climb up, I beg you, to the top of the tower to see whether my brothers are coming. They promised to come and see me today, so if you see them, signal to them to make haste.'

Her sister Anne went up to the top of the tower, and the wretched girl called up to her from time to time, 'Anne, sister Anne, do you see nothing coming?' And her sister replied, 'I see nothing but the dusty sunlight and the grass growing green.'

Meanwhile Bluebeard, holding a great cutlass in his hand, was shouting with all his might to his wife, 'Come down quickly or I shall come up to you.'

'Just one moment more, I beg you,' replied his wife, and straight away she called to her sister, but in an undertone, 'Anne, sister Anne, do you see nothing coming?' And sister Anne replied, 'I see nothing but the dusty sunlight and the grass growing green.'

'Come down, I say, and quickly,' shouted Blue-beard, 'or I shall come up.'

'I'm coming,' she replied, and then she called again, 'Sister Anne, sister Anne, do you see nothing coming?'

'I see,' replied sister Anne, 'a great cloud of dust which is coming this way.'

'Is it my brothers?'

'Alas, no, my sister, it's a flock of sheep.'

'Will you not come down?' shouted Bluebeard.

'In just a moment,' replied his wife, and then she called, 'Anne, sister Anne, do you see nothing coming?'

'I see,' she replied, 'two horsemen coming this way but they are still far off . . . God be praised,' she added after a pause, 'they are my brothers, I am making signs to them to hurry as fast as they can.'

Bluebeard started to shout so loud that the whole house shook. The poor woman came down and threw herself at his feet, all in tears and her hair dishevelled.

'That will serve no purpose,' said Bluebeard, 'you must die.' Then, seizing her by the hair with one hand and with the other brandishing his cutlass in the air, he was about to chop off her head. The wretched woman, turning her face to him and looking at him with dying eyes, begged him to allow her a moment to prepare her thoughts for death.

'No, no,' he said, 'commend your soul to God,' and raising his arm . . .

Just at that second there was such a loud banging at the door that Bluebeard stopped short. The door was flung open and in came two horsemen who, sword in hand, rushed straight at Bluebeard. He recognized them as his wife's brothers, one a dragoon, the other a musketeer, and he tried to run away and make his escape, but the two brothers pursued him so closely that they caught him before he was able to reach the steps of the porch. They ran their swords through his body and left him dead.

The poor woman was almost as dead as her husband, and had not the strength to get up to embrace her brothers.

It turned out that Bluebeard had no heirs, and so his wife was left mistress of all his possessions. She used part of them to arrange a marriage between her sister and a young gentleman who had long been in love with her. Another portion she used to purchase a captain's commission for each of her brothers, and the remainder for her own marriage to a most worthy gentleman who enabled her to forget the evil time she had spent with Bluebeard.

CHARLES PERRAULT

The Three Sillies

Once upon a time there was a farmer and his wife who had one daughter, and she was courted by a gentleman. Every evening he used to come and see her, and stop to supper at the farmhouse, and the daughter used to be sent down into the cellar to draw the beer for supper. So one evening she had gone down to draw the beer, and she happened to look up at the ceiling while she was drawing, and she saw a mallet stuck in one of the beams. It must have been there a long, long time, but somehow or other she had never noticed it before, and she began a-thinking. And she thought it was very dangerous to have that mallet there, for she said to herself: 'Suppose him and me was to be married, and we was to have a son, and he was to grow up to be a man, and come down into the cellar to draw the beer, like as I'm doing now, and the mallet was to fall on his head and kill him, what a dreadful thing it would be!' And she put down the candle and the jug, and sat herself down and began a-crying.

Well, they began to wonder upstairs how it was that she was so long drawing the beer, and her mother went down to see after her, and she found her sitting on the settle crying, and the beer running over the floor. 'Why, whatever is the matter?' said her mother. 'Oh, Mother!' says she, 'look at that horrid mallet!

Suppose we was to be married, and was to have a son, and he was to grow up, and was to come down to the cellar to draw the beer, and the mallet was to fall on his head and kill him, what a dreadful thing it would be!' 'Dear, dear! what a dreadful thing it would be!' said the mother, and she sat her down aside of the daughter and started a-crying too. Then after a bit the father began to wonder that they didn't come back, and he went down into the cellar to look after them himself, and there they two sat a-crying, and the beer running all over the floor. 'Whatever is the matter?' says he. 'Why,' says the mother, 'look at that horrid mallet. Just suppose, if our daughter and her sweetheart was to be married, and was to have a son, and he was to grow up, and was to come down into the cellar to draw the beer, and the mallet was to fall on his head and kill him, what a dreadful thing it would be!' 'Dear, dear, dear! so it would!' said the father, and he sat himself down aside of the other two, and started a-crying.

Now the gentleman got tired of stopping up in the kitchen by himself, and at last he went down into the cellar, too, to see what they were after; and there they three sat a-crying side by side, and the beer running all over the floor. And he ran straight and turned the tap. Then he said: 'Whatever are you three doing, sitting there crying, and letting the beer run all over the floor?' 'Oh!' says the father, 'look at that horrid mallet! Suppose you and our daughter was to be married, and was to have a son, and he was to grow up, and was to come down into the cellar to draw the beer, and the mallet was to fall on his head and kill him!' And then they all started a-crying worse than before. But the gentleman burst out a-laughing, and reached up and pulled out the mallet, and then he said: 'I've travelled many miles, and I never met three such big sillies as you three before; and now I shall start out on my travels again, and when I can find three bigger sillies than you three, then I'll come back and marry your daughter.' So he wished them good-bye, and started off on his travels, and left them all crying because the girl had lost her sweetheart.

Well, he set out, and he travelled a long way, and at last he came to a woman's cottage that had some grass growing on the roof. And the woman was trying to get her cow to go up a ladder to the grass, and the poor thing durst not go. So the gentleman asked the woman what she was doing. 'Why, lookye,' she said, 'look at all that beautiful grass. I'm going to get the cow on to the roof to eat it. She'll be quite safe, for I shall tie a string round her neck, and pass it down the chimney, and tie it to my wrist as I go about the house, so she can't fall off without my knowing it.' 'Oh, you poor silly!' said the gentleman, 'you should cut the grass and throw it down to the cow!' But the woman thought it was easier to get the cow up the ladder than to get the grass down, so she pushed her and coaxed her and got her up, and tied a string round her neck, and passed it down the chimney, and fastened it to her own wrist. And the gentleman went on his way, but he hadn't gone far when the cow tumbled off the roof, and hung by the string tied round her neck, and it strangled her. And the weight of the cow tied to her wrist pulled the woman up the chimney, and she stuck fast half-way and was smothered in the soot.

Well, that was one big silly.

And the gentleman went on and on, and he went to an inn to stop the night, and they were so full at the inn that they had to put him in a double-bedded room, and another traveller was to sleep in the other bed. The other man was a very pleasant fellow, and they got very friendly together; but in the morning, when they were both getting up, the gentleman was surprised to see the other hang his trousers on the knobs of the chest of drawers and run across the room and try to jump into them, and he tried over and over again and couldn't manage it; and the gentleman wondered whatever he was doing it for. At last he stopped and wiped his face with his handkerchief. 'Oh dear,' he says, 'I do think trousers are the most awkwardest kind of clothes that ever were. I can't think who could have invented such things. It takes me the best part of an hour to get into mine every morning, and I get so hot! How do you manage yours?' So the gentleman burst out a-laughing, and showed him how to put them on; and he was very much obliged to him, and said he never should have thought of doing it in that way.

So that was another big silly.

Then the gentleman went on his travels again; and he came to a village, and outside the village there was a pond, and round the pond was a crowd of people. And they had got rakes, and brooms, and pitchforks reaching into the pond; and the gentleman asked what was the matter. 'Why,' they say, 'matter enough! Moon's tumbled into the pond, and we can't rake her out anyhow!' So the gentleman burst out a-laughing, and told them to look up into the sky, and that it was only the shadow in the water. But they wouldn't listen to him, and abused him shamefully, and he got away as quick as he could.

So there was a whole lot of sillies bigger than them

three sillies at home. So the gentleman turned back home again and married the farmer's daughter, and if they didn't live happy for ever after, that's nothing to do with you or me.

JOSEPH JACOBS

Puss in Boots

There once lived a miller who had three children and all he could leave them when he died was his mill, his donkey and his cat. The share-out was quickly done, and no lawyer or solicitor was called in, for if they had been, they would very soon have eaten up the slender legacy. The eldest son had the mill, the second the donkey, and the youngest was left with only the cat, and he was none too pleased with such a miserable portion.

'My brothers,' he said, 'could well earn a decent living by putting their inheritance together, but as for me, when I've eaten my cat and made a muff out of its skin, I shall die of hunger.' The cat, who overheard what he had said but pretended not to, said to him in a grave and serious tone, 'Don't be downcast, master. Just give me a bag and have a pair of boots made for me so that I can get through the brambles and woods, and you'll find that your share has not been as bad as you believe.'

Although the cat's master did not attach too much importance to what he said, he had seen him play so many wily tricks in catching rats and mice, such as suspending himself by his feet or pretending to be dead when he hid in the flour, that he did not altogether despair of being helped out of his misery by the cat.

197

When the cat had got what he'd asked for, he looked the picture of elegance with his new boots. Slinging the bag round his neck and using his front paws to pull the drawstrings, he padded off to a warren where there were a great number of rabbits. Putting some bran, endive and chicory into his bag and lying down at full length as though he were dead, he waited for some young rabbit, unused to the tricks of this world, to stick its head into the bag to eat what he'd put into it.

No sooner had he lain down than he got what he wanted. A scatterbrained young rabbit went into the bag and Master Puss, pulling the strings tight, took it and killed it without mercy. Filled with pride at his capture, he went off to the king and requested to speak to him. He was shown upstairs to His Majesty's apartment, where, upon entering and making a low bow to the king, he said, 'May I offer you, Sire, a rabbit from the warren of my master, the Marquis of Carabas, which he has asked me to present to you on his behalf.' (Puss had decided to confer on his master the title of Marquis of Carabas.)

'Pray inform your master,' replied the king, 'that I thank him and accept the gift with great pleasure.'

Another time the cat went and hid himself in the corn with his bag open, and when two partridges had got in he pulled the strings and captured both of them, just as he had done with the rabbit. The king accepted them with great pleasure and sent him off with money to buy himself a drink.

For two or three months the cat went on offering the king presents of game from time to time, as if they came from his master. One day, when he knew that the king would be taking a drive along the riverside with his daughter, the most beautiful princess in the world, he said to his master, 'If you are prepared to follow my advice, your fortune is made. All you have to do is to go and bathe in the river, at a spot which I will point out to you, and leave the rest to me.'

The marquis did as his cat advised without understanding what use it could be. While he was bathing, the king came by and the cat began to cry at the top of his voice, 'Help! Help! My lord, the Marquis of Carabas, is drowning!' Hearing this cry, the king put his head out of the carriage window and, recognizing the cat who had brought him gifts of game so many times, he ordered his guards to hasten quickly to the rescue of the Marquis of Carabas. While they were pulling the poor 'marquis' out of the river, the cat came up to the carriage and told the king that while his master was bathing, thieves had run off with his clothes, although he had shouted 'Stop thief' with all his might (in fact that rogue of a cat had hidden the clothes under a large stone). The king commanded his gentlemen of the wardrobe to fetch some of his finest clothes for his lordship the marquis. His Majesty showed the young man a thousand signs of affection, and since the fine clothes suited him excellently (for he was indeed handsome and well-made) the king's daughter found him very much to her liking. Hardly had the marquis thrown her two or three highly respectful and somewhat tender glances when she fell madly in love with him. The king invited him to join him in his carriage and be part of the procession. The cat, delighted to see that his plan was beginning to succeed, walked on in front and meeting some peasants who were mowing a meadow said to them, 'My good people mowing the meadow, if you fail to tell the king that this meadow belongs to his lordship the Marquis of Carabas you will all be chopped up as fine as mincemeat.'

The king did not fail to ask the mowers to whom the meadow they were mowing belonged.

'It belongs to my lord the Marquis of Carabas,' they replied in unison, for the cat's threat had frightened them.

'You have a splendid domain here,' said the king to the marquis.

'Yes, Sire,' replied the marquis, 'and it is a meadow which unfailingly yields a plentiful harvest every year.'

Master Puss, who was still in front of them, met some reapers and said to them, 'You good folk who are reaping, if you do not say that all this corn belongs to the Marquis of Carabas you will all be chopped up as fine as mincemeat.'

The king passed by a few moments later and desired to know to whom all that corn belonged. 'It belongs to my lord the Marquis of Carabas,' replied the reapers and the king congratulated the marquis once again.

The cat, still walking in front of the carriage, continued to say the same sort of thing to all those whom he met, and the king was amazed at the vast estates of the Marquis of Carabas.

Master Puss came at last to a stately castle whose owner was an ogre, the richest ever known, for all the land through which the king had ridden was part of his domain. The cat, who had taken steps to find out who the ogre was and what exactly he was able to do, asked to speak with him, saying that he was reluctant to pass so close to the castle without having the honour of paying his respects. The ogre received him with as much civility as was within the nature of an ogre and invited him to take a rest.

'I have been assured,' began the cat, 'that you possess the gift of being able to change yourself into any sort of animal you please, for example, into a lion or an elephant.'

'That is true,' replied the ogre briskly, 'and to demonstrate that gift you will see me transform myself into a lion.'

The cat was so terrified at being confronted by a lion that he immediately made for the gutter on the roof, which was not without difficulty or peril, because his boots were of little use for walking on tiles.

Some time later, when he saw that the ogre had returned to his usual shape, the cat came down and confessed that he had been very much affrighted.

'I have also been assured,' he said, 'though I could scarcely bring myself to credit it, that you possess the power of assuming the shape of the smallest animal, for example, a rat or a mouse; I confess that to me it seems quite impossible.'

'Impossible?' rejoined the ogre. 'You'll see.' And at once he changed himself into a mouse, which went scampering along the floor. No sooner had the cat spotted it than he sprang upon it and devoured it.

Meanwhile the king saw the ogre's stately castle as he was riding past and wished to visit it. The cat, hearing the sound of the carriage as it crossed over the drawbridge, ran out to meet the king and said, 'Welcome, Your Majesty, to the castle of my lord the Marquis of Carabas.'

'What! My Lord Marquis,' exclaimed the king, 'is this castle too owned by you? Nothing could be more beautiful than this courtyard and all these splendid buildings surrounding it. If you please, let us go in and view the interior.'

The marquis gave his hand to the young princess and followed the king. They entered a large hall, where they found a magnificent feast which the ogre had prepared for his friends who were due to visit him that very day but who had not dared to enter, knowing that the king was there. His Majesty was quite charmed by the Marquis's excellent qualities, no less than his daughter, who had already fallen hopelessly in love with him. Having seen the vast estates which he owned and drunk five or six glasses of wine, the king said to him, 'If you do not become my son-in-law the fault will lie only with you.' The marquis, bowing low several times, accepted the honour which the king was bestowing upon him and that very day he was wedded to the princess. Puss became a great lord and no longer chased mice except for amusement.

CHARLES PERRAULT

Midas and the Golden Touch

In the time of the ancient Greeks King Midas ruled over the land of Phrygia. He was a good king and the people loved him.

Midas's palace was famed for its riches and more especially for its rose gardens. Visitors would come from far and wide to catch a glimpse of the splendid blooms and delicate hues and to breathe their fragrant scents.

Since Midas was exceedingly rich, his palace was naturally of the utmost splendour. Its pillars were golden and its lavish furnishings were all inlaid with gold. His tableware and drinking-cups were of gold and even his singing bird lived in an elaborate golden cage. The throne from which he gave his royal commands was of solid gold. His robes were of the finest cloth, spun from shimmering gold thread. His golden carriage was so grand that people lined the streets to gaze upon it open-mouthed as he rode forth each morning from the palace.

Midas loved gold. It was his one weakness. His desire for it grew stronger from day to day till it all but took possession of him. He wanted more gold, and more, and more, and still more.

He began to spend most of his time in his treasure vaults, counting the precious coins and lovingly fingering the golden jewellery, all the while gazing in

an ecstasy of pleasure at all his other precious gems –
the rubies, the amethysts, the sapphires and emeralds
which filled his vast chests to overbrimming. He even
took to locking himself in, alone and uninterrupted,
under the spell of these gleaming possessions as they
glittered in the sunlight peeping through the narrow
chinks of his vaults.

King Midas had a little daughter whom he loved
more than anything in the world. Her golden tresses
fell round her pretty little face, and an entrancing
picture she made as she frolicked merrily round her
father's throne or skipped alongside him as he strolled
through the palace gardens with their profusion of
roses. She thought they were the loveliest flowers in
the world when he picked her up for her to breathe her
full share of their scent. And she would dance and
sing as they made their way by the stream that flowed
through the rose gardens.

One morning the gardeners came across an old man
asleep in a drunken stupor on the grass. They bound
him with garlands of flowers and carried him to the
king. Midas at once recognized his prisoner – none
other than the jolly Silenus, rubicund and rotund. He
had been tutor to the god Dionysus, the god of wine;
Silenus was one of his faithful band of followers and
his very dear friend. Midas, too, was a great admirer of
Dionysus and was honoured to have a friend of his in
his palace. He invited Silenus to be his guest, and for
ten days he wined and dined and entertained him
with all manner of delightful amusements. And during this time Silenus told his host all manner of tales of
wondrous lands far away across the seas. And Midas
was enchanted.

At the end of that time Silenus was escorted back to

Dionysus, whose followers had been searching everywhere for him. So pleased was Dionysus to find his lost
companion that he sent a messenger to Midas in-
dicating that he would grant him any reward he chose
to name. 'The god Dionysus,' the messenger announced,
'bade me warn you to make your wish wisely and to
think carefully before you do so. What, then, oh King
Midas, shall I tell the god is your dearest wish?'

Midas thought and thought, but his every thought
could turn on only one thing and one thing only –
GOLD. If he could *make* gold, he could have veritable
mountains of it, reaching up to the skies. So, boldly,
without further hesitation, he proclaimed his most
heartfelt desire. 'Tell the great Dionysus that Midas
wishes to possess the Golden Touch, so that anything
he touches will turn to gold. If this wish is fulfilled he
will be the happiest man in the world.'

When Dionysus heard this wish he sighed, but
nevertheless he kept his promise. He dispatched his
messenger back to King Midas with these words,
'Tomorrow at sunrise you will find yourself endowed
with the Golden Touch.'

Hardly had night given way to dawn when Midas,
who had not slept a wink all night, decided to test
Dionysus's promised gift. He stretched out his eager
hand and touched everything in reach that wasn't
already gold – a chair, a flower-vase, a silken cushion –
but was bitterly disappointed to find that they
remained completely unchanged. He lay back on his
bed, as miserable as though he had been the poorest
man in the world. He had worked himself up to such a
pitch of excited expectation that he felt he could not
live if this Golden Touch were denied him. He gazed
gloomily out at the grey skies . . . then, suddenly, he

sprang up in stunned amazement. With the first rays of the rising sun the bed-covers he was touching had been transformed into a texture of the purest gold. As he drew back the curtains around his bed, he saw that they too had been transmuted into gold.

In a frenzy of excitement Midas rushed down the carpeted staircase, each step as he trod on it changing into the coveted metal. The banister, as his hand skimmed it, became a bar of burnished gold.

Then out into the palace grounds – he couldn't wait to see a forest of golden trees – and next to his roses, his exquisite roses. With one feather touch each bloom hardened into a golden rose, its delicate petals inclining to the gilded stem. Even the veins on the leaves stood out boldly in golden relief. He plucked an apple from a golden branch and gazed in wonder at its little gold stalk as he felt the golden roundness of it in his palm.

He walked with silent bliss up the now golden steps to his palace, turning walls, corridors and alcoves to the metal of his desire. But he was ready now to eat a hearty breakfast. He sat down at the table to await, as usual, the arrival of his little daughter. To his great surprise, however, and as an unpleasant awakening from his day-dream, he was distressed to see her looking more miserable than he had ever seen her and actually crying. Midas, thinking to cheer her up, leaned across the table to touch her little bowl and transform it into glistening gold. Now this bowl was much loved by his daughter, for its quaint little figures and pretty flowers arranged around the top rim gave her great delight to pore over when she had finished her food. 'But when it is golden,' thought Midas, 'she will love it even more.'

207

'What is it, my dear daughter, that saddens you and makes you sob so piteously?' he asked. She held out one of the roses which Midas had so recently changed to gold. 'It's horrid, it's hard and ugly,' she sobbed. 'I can't smell its lovely scent. I ran out into the garden to gather a sweet bunch of roses for you – I know how much you love them – but they had all turned this nasty yellow colour and they are no longer soft and velvety. What's happened to our roses? Where's their perfume gone?'

Midas tried hard to comfort his little daughter. 'Eat your breakfast, my dear, and afterwards I shall explain it all to you and you will be the happiest little girl in the world.'

Midas reached out for a piece of bread, but before he had broken it, it had changed to gold and the hard metal jarred his teeth. He raised his goblet to sip a little wine, but his delight at feeling the goblet turn to gold was instantly destroyed when unpleasant molten gold touched his lips. He transferred some meat to his plate with his fork, thinking that the fork would come between his teeth and the food, but again he found his teeth meeting the hard metal. His throat was parched with thirst and he was feeling very hungry indeed. 'I shall die of starvation,' he thought with terror. In desperation he grabbed at a large plum, stuffing it into his mouth, stone and all, thinking that speed would be the answer to his Golden Touch – beating it at its own game. But to no avail. Before a single drop of its delicious juice could ooze on to his palate, the plum was as hard as the metal it had now changed into.

Such a sumptuously appetizing breakfast-table – a table groaning with the choicest meats and fruits, bread, wine and sweetmeats – and not one single thing could he eat or drink. The poor man was terrified. What would become of him? Here he was with the gift that would make him the richest king in the world, yet not a bite to be eaten or a drop to be drunk. He would surely die.

He looked helplessly at his little daughter, who had just finished her food and was staring in dismay at her bowl, whose pretty figures stared metallically back at her. But as she waited for her father to explain it all, the little girl could see that he was in a state of extreme distress. It dawned on her that something dreadful had happened.

'Father, dearest father,' she cried, running up to him, 'what is it? What is the matter?' She threw her arms around his neck while he hugged and kissed her. At that moment he felt that his daughter's love was worth infinitely more than the Golden Touch. 'My little one!' he cried. But the little one made no response, nor did she stir. Nor could she. For the moment she had flung herself into his arms and his lips had touched her forehead she had become a cold, gold statue. Her golden curls now hung stiffly round her little golden face. The tears on her cheeks had congealed. He held her in his arms but her little body was no longer soft.

Midas raised his arms in horror and cried out in agony to the gods, begging forgiveness for his stupid greed for gold.

The god Dionysus heard Midas's cry of despair and could not refrain from mocking him for the folly of his wish. Yet he did feel sympathy for the mortal who would now gladly have forfeited every grain of gold in the world if he could only have restored the cold gold little figure in his arms to her soft warm self.

So once more Dionysus sent down his messenger to the king. 'Oh, rid me of this accursed gift!' cried Midas in anguish as soon as he appeared, tearing in frenzy at the roots of his hair – which, of course, stiffened as he did so. 'Pray tell the great Dionysus that I rue to the very depths of my being the arrant stupidity of my wish and repent the choice that I so greedily made. I have lost that which means more to me than anything in this life. If he will deign to help me regain my normal mortal powers, never again will I crave for those things which I do not deserve.'

And the messenger's reply was: 'Dionysus has forgiven you, for he knows of your suffering. Go down, therefore, to the River Pactolus and follow it till you reach its source near Mount Timolus. There, where the foaming waters come gushing from the rocks, bathe yourself in the river. The gold will be utterly cleansed from your body and the gift of the Golden Touch will be taken from you. Carry pitchers of these waters and pour them plentifully upon anything you wish to be changed to its erstwhile form.'

Scarcely were the words out of the messenger's mouth when Midas grabbed the largest of the pitchers he could lay his hands on and dashed headlong towards the turbulent waters of the Pactolus. He plunged deep into the rushing river till the gold of his body had turned the sand of the river into sparkling grains. To this very day the sands of that river have retained their golden hue.

Midas felt cleansed not only in body but in heart and mind too. He felt his foolish greed had been washed away together with his Golden Touch. Filling his pitcher, he rushed with all speed to the palace and poured it full over the golden figure of his adored daughter. Her hair softened into falling glinting tresses round her little round face, now flushed and rosy. She laughed heartily to see her father pouring water all over her, drenching her pretty dress. And Midas, dripping from head to foot, joined in the merriment, his laughter resonant with gratitude and relief. 'Father dear,' said the child, 'what *are* you doing?' for she had no notion that seconds earlier she had been a lifeless statue.

Midas took her little hand in his and together they splashed water on all the golden roses; how they glowed at the sight of their return to their natural beauty as the exquisite fragrance filled the air around them. Midas sprinkled water over everything his Golden Touch had transformed into the now hated metal until they were all as they had been before.

Soon the king was seated in dry royal robes at the table beside his little daughter, as pretty as a picture, in her clean little dress, and they ate the heartiest breakfast ever enjoyed by a king and princess or, for that matter, by any ordinary being on earth.

retold by STEPHEN CORRIN

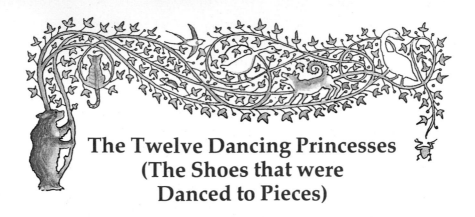

The Twelve Dancing Princesses
(The Shoes that were
Danced to Pieces)

There was once a king who had twelve daughters, each one more beautiful than the next. They slept together in one room where their beds stood in a row, and in the evening, when they lay down, the king locked the door and bolted it. But when he unlocked the door next morning he saw that their shoes were worn right through with dancing, and nobody could think how that had come about. Then the king issued a proclamation that whoever could find out where they had danced in the night could choose one of them as his wife and become king after his death. But if anyone presented himself and had not solved the mystery after three days and nights, then he should forfeit his life.

In due course a king's son presented himself and volunteered to take the risk. He was given a warm welcome, and in the evening he was taken to a room adjoining the bedroom of the princesses. A bed was set up for him there, and he was to keep watch to see where they went and where they danced. And in order that they shouldn't do anything in secret or leave their room, the doors between the rooms were left open. But after a while the eyes of the king's son began to feel as heavy as lead, and he dozed off. And when he awoke in the morning, he saw that all twelve had been dancing, for there were their shoes with holes in the soles. It was no different on the second and third night, and so the king's son was beheaded without mercy. After this many more suitors came forward to risk their lives in this daring adventure, but there wasn't one that did not end up dead.

Now it so happened that a poor soldier, who had been wounded in battle and was no longer fit for service, found himself on the road to the city where the king dwelt. He chanced to meet an old woman, who asked him where he was bound for.

'I don't quite know the answer to that myself,' he replied, and then, half-jokingly, he added, 'I'd like to find out where the king's daughters dance their shoes out. Then, one day, who knows, I might wear the king's crown.'

'Well, it's not as hard as all that,' said the old woman. 'You must avoid drinking the wine the princesses will bring you in the evening, and then pretend you're sound asleep.' Whereupon she gave him a little cloak, saying, 'When you wrap this around yourself you'll be invisible and then you'll be able to follow the twelve princesses.'

With the benefit of this good advice, the soldier took his courage in both hands and presented himself before the king as a suitor.

He was well received, like all the others, and was given princely garments to put on. In the evening, when it was time to go to bed, he was led to the adjoining room, and the eldest of the princesses brought him a cup of wine. But the soldier had tied a sponge under his chin; he allowed the wine to run into the sponge and did not drink a single drop. Then he lay down and after a while began to snore as though he were sleeping like a log. The king's twelve daughters heard him snore and laughed. The eldest sister said, 'There goes another who has thrown away his life.' Then they got up, opened cupboards, chests and cases, and brought out some splendid dresses. They smartened themselves up in front of mirrors, and jumped about the room, looking forward to the dance. Only the youngest said, 'I don't know why you're all making so merry; I've got this odd feeling that there's some bad luck coming our way.'

'You're a silly goose,' said the eldest, 'you're always fearful something bad is going to happen. Have you forgotten how many princes have already watched us in vain? Even if I hadn't bothered to give the soldier the sleeping potion, the silly oaf would still be dead asleep.' When they were ready, they had another look at the soldier, but his eyes were closed tight, and he didn't stir a muscle, and so they thought they were perfectly safe. Then the eldest went to her bed and struck it hard; straight away it sank into the ground, and they all followed it down through the opening, one after the other, the eldest in front. The soldier, who had watched everything, didn't waste any time, wrapped his cloak around him and went down after the youngest princess. But about half-way down, on the steps, he trod on her gown. She was frightened and cried out, 'What's that! Who's pulling on my dress?'

'Don't be so silly!' said the eldest. 'You must have caught it on a hook.'

So they continued down all the steps, and when they were at the bottom, they were in a wonderful avenue of trees where all the leaves were of silver, gleaming and glittering. The soldier thought to himself, 'I'd better get some evidence of this to take back

214

with me,' and so he broke off one of the branches. There followed a mighty cracking noise from the tree and the youngest princess cried out again, 'Something's wrong! Didn't you hear that noise?' The eldest princess replied, 'Those are salvoes of joy because we have set our princes free once again.'

Then they came to an avenue of trees where all the leaves were of gold and finally to a third avenue where they were shining diamonds. The soldier tore off a bunch from both of these, and each time there was a crack so that the youngest princess collapsed from fright. But the eldest sister insisted that the sounds were only salvoes of rejoicing.

They went on further until they came to a great stretch of water on which were twelve little boats, and in each boat sat a handsome prince. They had been expecting the princesses, and each prince took a sister into his boat, but the soldier got in with the youngest. Then the prince said, 'I don't understand, the boat is much heavier today. I have to row with all my strength if I'm to keep moving.'

'It must be the warm weather,' said the princess. 'I'm feeling very hot myself.'

Now on the other side of the water stood a beautiful, brightly illuminated castle from which came joyous resounding music of drums and trumpets. They rowed across to it, went in, and each prince danced with his chosen princess. The soldier, however, quite invisible, danced alone, and when one of the princesses took a cup of wine he drank it up so that it was empty when she put it to her lips. The youngest was quite upset by this, but her eldest sister always contrived to calm her.

And so they went on dancing till three o'clock in the

morning, and by then all their slippers had been danced right through and the dancing had to stop.

The princes took them back across the water in the boats, but this time the soldier sat in front, next to the eldest princess. When they reached the bank they said farewell to the princes and promised they would come again the next night. When they reached the stairs, the soldier ran on ahead and got into his bed, and when the twelve princesses climbed, slow and weary, up the steps, he was already snoring so loudly that they could all hear him, and they told one another, 'We're safe from that one.' Then they took off their beautiful dresses, put them away, placed their danced-out shoes under the bed and went to sleep.

The next morning the soldier didn't wish to say anything; he only wanted to see the wonderful things happening again, and so he went with the twelve princesses on the second and third nights. It all happened again, just as it had on the first night – the princesses danced their slippers right through just as before. On the third visit, however, he took the drinking cup as a proof.

When the time came for him to make his answer before the king, he tucked away the three branches and the cup and stood before him, while the twelve sisters stood hidden behind the door and listened to what he would say.

When the king put the question, 'Where have my twelve daughters been dancing their shoes out in the night?' the soldier replied, 'With twelve princes in an underground castle,' and he went on to relate how it had all taken place, and displayed the branches and the cup as proof.

The king then sent for his daughters and asked them

216

if what the soldier had reported was true, and since they could see that they had been discovered and that telling lies would be no use, they had to admit everything. Then the king asked the soldier which one he would take as his wife and he replied, 'I'm not so young any more, so I'll take the eldest.' And so, on that very same day, the wedding was celebrated and the kingdom was promised to him after the king's death.

As for the princes, however, they remained spellbound underground for as many more days as the number of nights they had danced with the twelve princesses.

THE BROTHERS GRIMM

The Emperor's New Clothes

Many years ago there was an Emperor who was so madly fond of elegant new clothes that he spent practically all his money trying to look well dressed. He didn't take much interest in his soldiers nor did he bother much about driving into the forest or going to the theatre, unless, of course, it was to show off his smart new clothes. For every hour of the day he had a different suit and if at any time you were to ask where he was, you would be sure to get the reply, 'The Emperor is in his dressing room,' and not – as you might expect – 'The Emperor is holding a meeting of his councillors.'

In the great city where he lived, life was always gay and lively, and the streets were crowded with visitors coming and going. One day two swindlers arrived in the city and told everyone willing to listen that they were weavers who could make the most beautiful cloth imaginable, with the most elaborate patterns and in the richest colours. And they also claimed that the material which they put into the clothes had a most remarkable quality – *it was invisible to anyone who was stupid, or unfit to hold his job.*

'These would indeed be fine clothes!' thought the Emperor. 'If I were wearing them I should be able to find out which men in my kingdom were unfit for the posts they held and I could distinguish the fools from the wise. I must have some clothes woven from this material without delay!' And he gave the two swindlers a large sum of money in advance so that they might begin work immediately. They set up two looms and pretended to be weaving, but in reality there was nothing at all on their looms. Then they demanded to be given the finest silk and the costliest gold thread – which they proceeded to put into their own pockets – and worked at the empty looms late into the night.

'I should really like to know how they are getting on with the cloth,' thought the Emperor after a couple of days, but the idea that anyone who was stupid or unfit to hold his job would not be able to see it made him feel rather uncomfortable. And though he was confident there was nothing to fear as far as he himself was concerned, he still decided it might be better if he sent someone else along first to see how matters stood. All the people in the city knew what wonderful powers the material possessed and everybody was eager to find out how clever or how stupid his neighbours turned out to be.

'I will send my honest old minister of state to the weavers,' thought the Emperor. 'He is the best person I know to judge how the stuff looks; he's got good sense and no man is more fit for his post than he is.'

So the worthy old minister went along to the hall where the two knaves were sitting and working – or rather pretending to work – at their empty looms. 'Heaven preserve us!' thought the old man with a start, opening his eyes very wide. 'I can't see anything at all!' But he didn't say a word about it.

The two cheats begged him to be good enough to come closer and asked him whether he did not think the design was most pleasing and the colours beautiful. They pointed to the empty looms and the poor old man stared and stared, but he could see nothing, nothing at all, for there was nothing there to see.

'Heaven help me!' he thought. 'Am I really so stupid? I have never thought so myself and I certainly am not going to let anyone else think so. Is it possible that I am not fit for my job? No, it would never do for anyone to find out that I could not see the stuff.'

'Well, sir, will you not say whether the material pleases you?' asked one of the weavers.

'Oh, it is most attractive, most charming!' answered the old minister, peering through his spectacles. 'What a magnificent pattern and what pleasing colours! Yes, I shall certainly tell the Emperor that I am most pleased with it.'

'That is very gratifying!' said the two swindlers, and then they gave names to the shades of colours they had used and described the rare pattern. The old minister listened most attentively, for he wanted to repeat it all when he went back to the Emperor. Which is what he did.

And now the two knaves asked for more money and yet more silk and gold thread, which they said they needed for their weaving. They stuffed it all into their own pockets and not a single thread was put on the loom. Then, as before, they went on working at their empty looms.

Shortly after, the Emperor sent another honest official to see how the weavers were getting on with their work and whether the cloth would soon be ready. Exactly the same happened with him as with the old minister. He just stood and stared, but as there wasn't anything at all on the bare looms he couldn't see anything.

'It really is a most beautiful piece of cloth, is it not?' asked the swindlers, pointing out the intricate patterns, and asking him to admire the exquisite colours that weren't there.

'Stupid I most certainly am not,' thought the man. 'Perhaps I am not fit for my job. It is quite ridiculous, and anyway I must not let it be known.' And so he praised the material which he couldn't see and declared his satisfaction with the rich colours and wonderful patterns.

To the Emperor he said: 'Yes, the weavers are doing a remarkable job. The cloth is exquisite.'

All the people in the city were talking of the magnificent cloth, and at last the Emperor decided he must go and see for himself while the material was still on the loom. Accompanied by a number of specially selected officials, among whom were the two who had already seen it, he went along to the two cunning knaves, who were weaving away for all they were worth without thread or fibre.

'Is not the work truly magnificent?' asked the two officials who had already been there. 'Just examine the pattern, Your Majesty, and the exquisite colours.' And they pointed to the empty loom, for they thought the others could see.

'What's the meaning of this?' thought the Emperor. 'I can't see a thing! This is quite frightening! Am I stupid? Am I not fit to be Emperor? This is the greatest disaster that could happen to me!' But aloud he said, 'The cloth is most beautiful. It has Our highest approval.' And he kept nodding his head with satisfaction and gazing appreciatively at the empty loom. He would not, he could not, admit that he saw nothing. All the officials who were with him looked and looked but saw nothing, any more than the rest, but, aping their Emperor, they said, 'How beautiful it is!' And they advised him to have clothes made from this magnificent material and to wear them for the first time at the great procession which was soon to take place. 'Splendid! Magnificent! Exquisite!' were the words on everyone's lips and everybody seemed highly delighted. The Emperor presented each of the swindlers with the Cross of the Order of Chivalry to wear in his buttonhole and the title of Knight of the Loom.

The whole night long before the morning of the procession the rascals sat up and worked (or rather, pretended to), burning more than sixteen candles, so that people could see that they were hard at work to complete the Emperor's new clothes. They pretended to take the stuff down from the loom; they made cuts in the air with huge scissors; they sewed with needles that had no thread; and finally they said: 'Look! The Emperor's clothes are now ready!'

The Emperor came along with his high-born cavaliers and the two knaves raised one arm as though they were holding up something and said, 'See, here are the trousers! Here is the coat! Just look at the cloak!' and so on and so forth. 'The whole suit is as light as a spider's web. Your Majesty will not feel any weight at all, but that is just the beauty of it.'

'Yes indeed!' agreed all the cavaliers; but they couldn't see anything at all, for there was nothing to see.

'Would Your Imperial Majesty be graciously pleased to remove your clothes?' asked the knaves. 'Then we will fit on the new clothes in front of the great mirror.'

The Emperor took off all his clothes and the cheats

behaved exactly as though they were fitting him carefully with each garment of his new suit, even pretending to fasten the train, which was to be carried behind him in the procession, round his waist. Then the Emperor turned round and round before the mirror.

'How splendid Your Majesty looks! How beautifully the clothes fit!' they all exclaimed. 'What a design! What colours! How truly magnificent is the general effect!'

Then came this announcement from the Chief Master of Ceremonies: 'They are waiting outside with the canopy which will be borne above Your Majesty in the procession.'

'I am quite ready,' said the Emperor. 'Does it not fit well?' And once more he turned to the mirror, for he wished it to appear as though he were examining his ornate robes with great interest.

The chamberlains, who were to carry the Emperor's train, fumbled about on the ground with their hands as if they were picking up the ends of the mantle; they made as if they were holding something up in the air. They dared not let it be noticed that they could not see anything.

So the Emperor walked in procession under the magnificent canopy and all the people in the streets, as well as those looking out of their windows, said, 'How incomparably beautiful are the Emperor's new clothes!' 'What a magnificent train he has to his mantle!' 'How perfectly it all matches!' No one would let on that there was nothing at all to be seen, because by doing so they would have shown themselves to be fools or unfit to hold their posts. Never had the Emperor's clothes excited so much admiration!

'But the Emperor hasn't got on anything at all!' cried a little child.

'Good heavens!' exclaimed his father. 'Just listen to what the innocent child is saying!' And then everybody started whispering to one another what the child had said. The whispers grew louder and louder until the whole people said at last, 'But he hasn't got anything on!' And the Emperor got the uncomfortable feeling that what they were saying was only too true; but he thought, 'All the same, I must carry on with the procession.' And he drew himself up and walked proudly on, and the chamberlains held firmly on to the train that wasn't there at all.

HANS CHRISTIAN ANDERSEN

Beauty and the Beast

Once upon a time there lived an extremely rich merchant who had six children, three sons and three daughters. As he was a most sensible man, he saw to it that his children received the best education he could afford, with the most excellent of teachers.

His two elder daughters were good-looking enough, but the youngest was radiantly beautiful; when she was small people used to call her Beauty, and that was the name she came to be known by, which made her sisters very jealous. But not only was she more beautiful than her sisters, she was also kinder. The two elder ones were haughty and very proud of their wealth; they put on the airs of great ladies, refusing to accept visits from other merchants' daughters. Every day they would go to balls, to the theatre or for walks where they could be seen. They poked fun at their younger sister, who spent most of her time reading good books.

Since people knew that these girls were enormously rich, several well-to-do merchants were eager to marry them. But the two elder sisters let it be known that they would never consent to marry anyone other than a duke or at least a count. Beauty thanked her suitors courteously but told them she was much too young to marry and that she wished to stay with her father for a few years more.

Then it happened that quite unexpectedly the merchant lost all his fortune and property, and all he had left was a small cottage in the country, a long way from town. With tears in his eyes he told his children that they would now have to move to this country cottage and that, by working hard, they might be able to eke out a living. The two elder girls announced that they had no wish to leave town; they knew many young men who would be only too happy to marry them even though they now had no fortune.

But these young ladies were mistaken; now that they were poor their former friends no longer acknowledged them. And, as everybody disliked them because of their pride, people said they didn't deserve to be pitied. 'We are only too glad,' they said, 'to see them taken down a peg. Let's see them play the fine lady while tending the sheep!' At the same time, people said how sorry they were for Beauty's misfortune. 'She's such a dear girl, she always spoke so kindly to poor folk, and she's so gentle and honest.'

There were several men of high birth who wanted to marry her even though now she did not have a penny to her name. But she always told them that she wouldn't think of leaving her poor father while he was in trouble and that she would follow him to the country to help him keep up his courage and assist him in his work.

When they were settled in their house in the country, the merchant and his three sons started working on the land. Beauty would get up at four in the morning, busying herself with cleaning the house and preparing meals for the family. She found this difficult at first and wept secret tears, for she wasn't used to working like a servant, but after a couple of months she found she was getting stronger and that the work was making her healthier. When she had done her day's work she would read, play the harpsichord and sit singing at her spinning-wheel.

Her two sisters, however, were bored by it all. They would get up at ten in the morning, take walks all day, and complain about missing their friends and not having the fine clothes and the grand carriage they were used to.

'Just look at our young sister,' they would say to each other. 'She's stupid enough to be happy with this wretched situation.'

The good merchant did not see things in this way. He knew that people found Beauty much more agreeable to be with than her sisters. He admired all her fine qualities, especially her patience, for her sisters simply watched her doing all the work and never missed a chance to insult her.

The family had been living like this for some time, cut off from society, when the merchant received a letter telling him that a ship bearing some of his merchandise, which he thought was lost, had just arrived safely in port. This news nearly turned the heads of the two elder girls, for they thought that at long last they would be able to give up their boring life in the country. When their father prepared to leave, they begged him to bring them back fine robes, furs, headdresses and all sorts of finery. But Beauty asked for nothing; she thought to herself that however much the merchandise might yield it would not be enough to satisfy her sisters' desires.

'Are you not asking me to buy you anything?' asked her father.

'Since you are so kindly thinking of me,' she

228

answered, 'I beg you to bring me back a rose, for there are none round here.'

It was not that Beauty cared so much for a rose, but she did not want to seem to criticize her sisters, who might have said that she was simply showing off by not asking for anything.

The good merchant took his leave of them and set out on his journey, but when he arrived at his destination he found only a small cargo and many people waiting to sue him for his merchandise, and after a great deal of trouble he set off for home as poor as he had been before. There were only thirty miles between him and his home, and he was already looking forward to seeing his children again. But there was a dense forest to be got through before he reached his house, and he lost his way. A terrible snow-storm arose and the wind blew so fiercely that twice it knocked him off his horse to the ground. As night fell he thought he would die of hunger or freeze to death, or that he might be devoured by the wolves which could be heard howling all around him.

Suddenly he espied a great light at the end of a long tree-lined drive, but it seemed so very, very far away. He walked towards where the light came from and saw that it shone from a grand castle, ablaze with light. The merchant gave thanks to God for the help he had sent him and made haste to reach the castle. But he was astonished at not meeting anyone in the court-yards. His horse was following behind him and, seeing a stable wide open, trotted in. There was plenty of hay and oats, and the wretched creature, almost starving, fell on them hungrily. The merchant tied it to a post in the stable and made his way to the house, where he found not a living soul. When he entered the great hall, he found a cheerful fire burning and a table laden with food, but a place laid only for one.

Soaked to the skin by rain and snow, he moved near the fire to get dry, saying to himself, 'The master of the house and his servants will surely forgive me the liberty I am taking and they will probably soon be coming in.' He waited a considerable time, but it struck eleven and no one had yet appeared; he could no longer still his hunger and helped himself to some chicken, which he gobbled down in two mouthfuls, all of a-tremble. He also drank a few glasses of wine and, becoming bolder, he left the hall and wandered through a number of large rooms, magnificently furnished. At last he came to a room containing a fine bed and, as it was past midnight and he was extremely weary, he closed the door and lay down to sleep. It was ten o'clock when he awoke next morning, and he was astonished to find that his own suit, which had been quite spoiled, had been replaced by a handsome new one. 'This place must no doubt belong to some good fairy who has taken pity on my sad situation,' he said to himself. He looked out of the window. The snow had vanished; beautiful beds of flowers met his enchanted gaze. He made his way into the great hall where he had supped the previous night and saw a small table with a pot of chocolate on it.

'I thank you, Madam Fairy,' he said aloud, 'for having so kindly thought of providing my breakfast.'

The good man drank the chocolate and went out to fetch his horse but, passing a bower of roses, he remembered that Beauty had asked him to bring her one. He plucked one small branch from among many others.

At that moment he heard a terrible noise and saw

coming towards him a Beast so frightful to look at that he nearly fell down in a faint.

'Ungrateful creature,' roared the Beast, 'I saved your life by receiving you into my castle, and in return you steal my roses, which I love more than anything else in the world. You will pay for this with your life. I will spare you a quarter of an hour to beg God's forgiveness.' The merchant fell on his knees and, clasping his hands, he addressed the beast: 'Pardon me, my Lord, I did not intend to offend you by taking a rose for one of my daughters; she desired me to bring her one.'

'I am not called "my Lord",' replied the monster, 'but "the Beast". I do not like compliments. I prefer people to speak their minds, so do not think you will move me by flattery. But you say you have daughters. I am willing to forgive you on condition that one of your daughters, of her own free will, comes here to die in your place. Let there be no discussion! Leave! And if your daughters refuse to die for you, swear to me that you will return within three months.'

The good man had no intention of sacrificing one of his daughters to the fearful beast, but he thought, 'At least I will have the pleasure of embracing them once more.' And so he swore he would come back and the Beast told him he could leave whenever he wished. 'But,' he added, 'I do not wish you to go away empty-handed. Return to the room where you slept and you will find there a large empty chest: you may put in it anything you please and I will see that it is sent to your home.'

The Beast then withdrew. The merchant consoled himself: 'If I must die,' he thought, 'I shall at least leave my poor children provided for.'

In the room where he had slept he saw the chest of which the Beast had spoken and filled it with a great quantity of gold coins which he also found there. He then went to fetch his horse from the stable and left the castle with a grief equal to the joy he had felt when entering it. His horse of his own accord chose the right road through the forest, and in a few hours the merchant arrived at his little cottage. His children gathered around him, but instead of showing any feeling for their caresses the merchant just looked at them and burst into tears. He was holding the spray of roses which he had brought for Beauty and, as he handed them to her, he said, 'Take these roses, Beauty! Your unhappy father has paid a high price for them.' And he went on to tell his family about the disaster which had befallen him.

When he had finished the two elder girls raised great cries and said insulting things to Beauty. But she did not weep.

'Just look what trouble this little creature's pride has brought upon us,' they said. 'Why didn't she ask for dresses just as we did! But no! Our miss had to show off. She will cause our father's death and she doesn't shed a single tear!'

'That would be quite useless,' replied Beauty. 'Why should I weep for my father's death? He is not going to die. Since the monster is willing to accept one of his daughters, I will surrender to his madness and will be happy to be his victim, since by doing so I shall save my father's life and prove my love for him.'

'No, sister,' said her three brothers. 'You shall not die. We shall hunt out the monster and perish by his blows if we cannot slay him.'

'There is no hope of doing that,' said their father.

'The power of the Beast is so great that we have no chance of putting an end to him. I am touched by Beauty's kind heart, but I cannot risk her death. I am an old man; I have only a short time to live. And so I shall lose only a few years of life which, dear children, I shall miss only because of you.'

'I assure you, dear Father,' said Beauty, 'you will not go back to the castle without me. And you cannot stop me from following you. Although I am young, I am not so much attached to life, and I would rather be devoured by that monster than die of the grief that your death would cause me.'

The merchant tried in vain to dissuade her from going, but Beauty had quite made up her mind to set out for the Beast's castle, and her sisters, of course, were delighted at the idea, because her goodness filled them with jealousy.

The merchant was so preoccupied with grief at the thought of losing his daughter that he quite forgot about the chest that he had filled with gold. But as soon as he had shut himself away in his room to retire he was astonished to find it at the foot of his bed. He decided to say nothing to his children or to tell them that he was now a rich man, because he knew his daughters would have wished to return to town, while he himself was resolved to spend his last years in the country. But secretly he told Beauty about it.

She told him that while he had been away two young men of high birth had visited them and had fallen in love with her sisters. She begged her father to let them get married without delay, for Beauty, in the kindness of her heart, was fond of them and forgave them for the wrongs they had done to her.

These wicked creatures rubbed onion on their eyes

233

to pretend to weep when Beauty left with her father. But her brothers' tears were real, as were her father's. Only Beauty herself did not cry, because she did not want to add to their sorrow.

Their horse took the road that led direct to the castle, and towards evening they saw it, all illuminated as on the first visit. The horse found his way alone to the stable, while the merchant and his daughter went into the great hall, where they found a table sumptuously laid for two. The good man hadn't the heart to eat, but Beauty, making a great effort to appear calm, sat down and served her father. She thought to herself, 'The Beast seems to have a mind to fatten me up before he eats me. That is why he has put on such a great banquet.'

When they had finished eating they heard a great noise. The merchant knew it was the Beast coming and with tears in his eyes he bade his daughter farewell. Beauty couldn't help shuddering at the sight of the Beast, but she tried her best to be calm and when he asked her if she had come of her own accord she replied in a trembling voice, 'Ye-es.'

'You are most kind,' the Beast said to her, 'and I am most obliged to you. And you, my good man,' he continued, turning to her father, 'you will leave tomorrow morning, and do not think of ever coming back. So, good-night to you.

'Good-night, Beauty,' he added, turning back to her.

'Good-night, Beast,' she replied, whereupon the monster withdrew.

'Ah! My daughter!' exclaimed the merchant, embracing Beauty. 'I am half dead with terror. Trust me, I beg you. Leave *me* here.'

234

'No, Father,' she replied firmly, 'you will leave tomorrow morning and entrust me to the mercy of Heaven.'

They went to bed not expecting any sleep that night, but scarcely were they in their beds when they fell into a deep sleep. In her sleep Beauty saw a lady who said to her, 'Beauty, your kind heart makes me happy. Your noble deed in giving your life to save your father will not go unrewarded.'

Beauty recounted her dream to her father when she awoke, and although it afforded him some consolation he could not help weeping his heart out when the moment came to be separated from his beloved daughter.

When he had left, Beauty sat down in the great hall and she too started to weep. But she soon plucked up courage and surrendered herself to the care of her Maker. She was determined not to grieve in the short time that was left to her to live, for she was convinced that the Beast would devour her that very evening. She decided to go for a walk round the beautiful castle.

She could not help admiring its splendour. But she was quite taken by surprise when she came upon a door with the words *Beauty's Room* written upon it. She hurriedly opened this door and was dazzled by the magnificence of all she saw inside. What struck her most was the large book-case, a harpsichord and several books of music.

'The Beast does not want me to become bored here,' she murmured, and then she thought, 'If I had only one day to spend here, he would surely not have provided me with all this,' and this idea inspired her with fresh courage. She opened the book-case and saw a book on which was written in letters of gold:

Beauty, queen of all you see,
Freely came you here to me.
Your wish comes true, be what it may,
You command and I obey.

'Alas,' she sighed, 'all I wish is to see my poor father and to know what he is doing at this moment.'

Imagine her astonishment when, glancing at a large mirror, she saw in it her house with her father just arriving and looking exceedingly sad. Her sisters were coming out to meet him and, despite the expressions they put on to pretend how grieved they were, the joy on their faces at the absence of their sister was unmistakable. After a moment it all vanished from the mirror, and Beauty couldn't help thinking that the Beast was most kindly, and that perhaps indeed she had nothing to fear from him.

At noon she found the table laid and while she ate, beautiful music played though no performer was visible. In the evening, as she was about to sit down to sup, she heard the loud noise that the Beast made and in spite of herself she trembled with fear.

'Beauty,' said the monster, 'may I have leave to watch you sup?'

'You are master here,' replied Beauty.

'No,' the Beast went on, 'you are mistress here, and you alone. Simply tell me to go away if my presence wearies you and I shall leave immediately. Tell me, though, do you not find me terribly ugly?'

'It's true, I do,' said Beauty. 'I cannot lie. But I think you are extremely kind.'

'What you say is right. But not only am I ugly, I am also stupid. I know only too well that I am only a beast.'

'People who are ready to say they are stupid are not stupid. A foolish person would never admit that he is a fool.'

'Please enjoy your supper, Beauty,' the Beast continued, 'and try to find pleasure in your new home, for everything here is yours and it would grieve me deeply to feel that you were not happy.'

'You are full of kindness,' said Beauty. 'I assure you that your goodness does make me happy. And when I think of that, you do not seem to be so ugly.'

'Ah,' said the Beast with a deep sigh, 'but I am still a monster even though I have a kind heart.'

'There are many men who are more of a monster than you,' said Beauty, 'and I would rather have you, despite your appearance, than those who, behind the face of a man, hide a false and ungrateful heart.'

'If I only knew how,' said the Beast, 'I would pay you a great compliment to express my thanks for saying those kind words. But I have little wit and all I can say is that I am most obliged to you.'

Beauty ate her supper and enjoyed it. She had almost lost her fear of the monster, but she nearly died of terror when he said to her, 'Beauty, would you consent to be my wife?'

For several moments no reply came from her lips; she was terrified in case she might arouse the monster's anger by refusing him. At last, in a trembling voice, she said simply, 'No, Beast.'

At these words the poor monster seemed to want to sigh but gave out such a frightful whistling sound that it re-echoed throughout the entire palace. But Beauty's mind was quickly put to rest, for the Beast, with the words, 'Farewell, then, Beauty,' went out of the room, turning round now and again to look at her. When she

was alone Beauty felt great pity for the poor creature. 'Alas,' she said, 'what a shame that such a kind creature should be so ugly.'

Beauty spent three tranquil months in the palace. Every evening the Beast visited her and talked with her as she ate her supper. What he said was quite good sense, but it was not what one might call intelligent conversation. But every day Beauty observed some new kindness in him, and as she became used to seeing him she also became accustomed to his ugliness. She no longer dreaded his appearance but rather found herself looking forward to nine o'clock, at which time the Beast never failed to arrive.

There was only one thing which upset Beauty; before going off to bed the Beast unfailingly asked her if she would consent to be his wife and would look utterly distressed when she said no.

At last one night she said to him, 'You sadden me, Beast. I should like to be able to marry you but I am too honest to let you believe that it will ever happen. I shall always be your friend; please try to let that make you happy.'

'If that must be so, I shall resign myself to it,' replied the Beast. 'I know I am hideous, but I love you very much. And indeed I am only too happy to know that you are content to remain here. Please promise me that you will never leave me.'

Beauty blushed at these words. She had seen in her mirror only that day that her father was pining away with sorrow at having lost her, and her great wish was to see him again.

'I could indeed promise never to leave you, but I so much wish to see my father again that I should die of grief if you refused me that wish.'

'I would rather die myself,' said the monster, 'than cause you grief. I will send you back to your father; you will stay with him and your poor Beast will die of sorrow.'

'No,' said Beauty with tears in her eyes. 'I am too fond of you to wish to cause your death. I promise you I will come back in a week's time. You have allowed me to see that my sisters are married and that my brothers have left for the army. My father is quite alone, let me stay with him only for a week.'

'You shall be with him tomorrow morning,' said the Beast. 'But remember your promise; when you want to come back here you will only have to place your ring on a table when you go to bed. That is all you will have to do. Farewell, Beauty.' As usual the Beast gave a deep sigh as he said these words, and Beauty went to her bed full of sorrow at having made him so sad.

When she awoke next morning she found she was in her father's house. She rang a little bell on her bedside table and a maid came in, uttering a great scream as she saw her. The good man came running in and nearly fainted with joy at the sight of his beloved daughter; he embraced her over and over again. After recovering from all this emotion Beauty realized she had no suitable clothes for getting up, but the maid told her she had just discovered in the adjoining room a large chest filled with dresses trimmed with gold and adorned with diamonds.

Beauty felt most grateful to the Beast for this considerate attention. She picked out the simplest gown and told the maid to pack the rest, for she wished to send them to her sisters. But she had scarcely uttered the words when the chest vanished. Her father said that perhaps the Beast wished her to keep all the dresses for herself and, in a flash, chest and dresses were back in the room where they were before.

When Beauty had dressed she was told that her sisters had arrived, accompanied by their husbands. Both of them were most unhappy. The elder one had married an exceedingly handsome man of noble birth, but he was so much in love with his own looks that he did nothing but study them from morning till night. The second had married a clever man who only used his cleverness to offend other people, including his own wife. Beauty's sisters nearly died of humiliation when they saw her dressed like a princess and looking more beautiful than a goddess. Nothing could quell their feelings of jealousy, which only increased when Beauty told them how happy she was. The two envious ladies went sobbing into the garden to vent their feelings.

'Why is that little creature happier than we are? Are we not more attractive than she?' they asked each other.

'An idea has just occurred to me,' said the elder. 'Let us try to detain her here for more than a week. That stupid Beast will be furious when he finds she has broken her word and maybe he will devour her.'

'You are right, sister,' said the other. 'Let's do everything we can to keep her here.'

Having decided on this they went back into the house and made a pretence of showing such kindness to Beauty that she wept with joy.

When the week had passed the two sisters tore their hair and pretended such grief when Beauty was about to leave that she promised to stay for another week. However, she felt guilty at the distress she must be causing to her poor Beast, for whom she felt a deep affection. Indeed, she found herself longing to see him again.

On the tenth night of her stay she dreamed she was in the palace garden, where the Beast lay dying on the lawn and with his last breath reminded her of her broken promise. Beauty awoke with a start and burst into tears.

'Is it not wicked of me,' she asked herself, 'to cause such great distress to a creature who has shown me such fond kindness? Is it his fault that he is so ugly and simple-minded? He is good and he is kind, and that is worth more than anything else. Why was I unwilling to be his wife? I should be happier with him than my sisters are with their husbands. It is neither beauty nor cleverness in a husband that makes a woman happy. What really matters is beauty of character and kindness. And the Beast has these qualities. I am not in love with him, but he has my respect, my gratitude and my friendship. I must *not* break his heart. If I did I should never forgive myself.' With these words Beauty rose and placed her ring on the table. Then she went back to bed and fell asleep almost immediately. To her great joy, when she woke up next morning she found herself in the Beast's palace. She dressed in her most magnificent clothes in order to give him pleasure and nearly died with impatience as she waited for the clock to strike nine. But the clock struck in vain, for the Beast did not appear at that hour. Beauty feared she might have caused his death, and in utter despair she ran screaming through the palace, 'Beast, dear Beast, where are you?' When she had searched through every possible place she remembered her dream and ran into the garden by the fountain where she had seen him in her sleep.

There she found the poor Beast lying unconscious. She thought he must be dead. She flung herself on his body, forgetting all her horror of his looks, and when she could feel his heart still beating she fetched water from the fountain and threw it over his face. The Beast opened his eyes and spoke. 'You forgot your promise, Beauty. I was so filled with grief at the thought that I might have lost you that I decided to starve myself to death. But I die happy in the pleasure of seeing you once again.'

'No, my dear Beast, you will not die!' said Beauty. 'You will live and be my husband. I offer you my hand, now, at this very moment. I give you my word that I will belong only to you. I thought, alas, that my feeling for you was only that of a friend, but the sorrow that I have felt has made me see that I could not live apart from you.'

No sooner were the words out of her mouth than the palace became ablaze with brilliant lights. Fireworks and music proclaimed a festive occasion. But none of this caught Beauty's eye. She was looking at her dear Beast, all a-tremble for his life. Impossible to describe her amazement when she saw that the Beast had disappeared and at her feet was a prince more handsome than anyone could imagine, who was thanking her for having broken a dread spell. 'But what has happened to my poor Beast?' she cried, gazing in utter amazement at the prince.

'You see him at your feet,' said the prince. 'A wicked fairy condemned me to assume that shape until a beautiful girl would consent to marry me, and she forbade me to show any sign of intelligence. And so you were the only one in the world who sensed my true character. I have always loved you, Beauty, and your love for me has broken the spell. I cannot repay you for all that you have done for me. Will you be my queen?'

Full of joyous astonishment, Beauty consented and she helped the handsome prince to his feet. Together they went to the palace and Beauty nearly died with pleasure when she saw in the great hall her father and the rest of her family, transported there by the same lady whom she had seen in her dream.

'Beauty,' said this lady, who was a celebrated fairy, 'receive the reward of your choice. You preferred noble character to either beauty or high intelligence and you deserve to find these qualities in one and the same person. Beauty, you will become a great queen.'

To the two sisters she said, 'I see inside your hearts and the malice within them. Your fate is to become two statues, but beneath the stone you will still retain your minds and feelings. You will remain at your sister's palace gates. Your only punishment will be to witness her happiness. Only when you are able to recognize the error of your ways will you be able to revert to your present shape. It is possible to free oneself from anger, greed, sloth and pride, but to get rid of a wicked and envious heart requires something of a miracle.'

And then, with a wave of her wand, everyone in the hall was transported to the prince's kingdom, where his subjects greeted him with joy.

He married Beauty and they lived together in happiness that was perfect because it was founded on goodness.

MADAME LE PRINCE DE BEAUMONT